D1733497

The steeples had made it possible for men to go to the stars. They built them thousands of miles up into the sky and then developed the drive that took them to the lights. A mixed blessing were the skyscrapers. First one, then dozens, then hundreds all sticking out into the endless night like beacons.

Everyone went away and the silence on the home-world was deafening. For a while. Out of obscurity things began to creep, crawl, fly and walk, things hidden since the species of man constructed his first weapons. There was no one to stop them from flourishing now, no one to say they couldn't grow and be openly active in their environment.

Now there was but one steeple remaining that could accommodate a landing craft. No one ever landed a ship on the ground, and after the last steeple became unsuitable men would never venture onto their home-world again. It wasn't nostalgia that made the powers on Laredo come up with Project Deep Green. Laredo wasn't large or hospitable enough so why not do a little meddling with Earth? After all it was so much closer than all the other worlds....

H.R. VAN DONGEN

EARTH IN TWILIGHT

Doris Piserchia

DAW BOOKS, INC.
DONALD A. WOLLHEIM, PUBLISHER

1633 Broadway, New York, N.Y. 10019

FIRST PRINTING, NOVEMBER 1981

1 2 3 4 5 6 7 8 9

DAW TRADEMARK REGISTERED
U.S. PAT. OFF. MARCA
REGISTRADA. HECHO EN U.S.A.

PRINTED IN U.S.A.

Chapter 1

The ship from the stars was coming down into the open mouth of the steeple, and Whing was excited because he was about to confront a spaceman. As far as he knew there hadn't been another of those specimens on Earth besides himself for a very long time.

He sped along a metal railing and hung out over the world to see if he alone was alerted to the impending landing. It seemed that he was. Earth looked like a big ball of yarn with a great many knitting needles sticking out of it. Loose yarn seemed to be strung from needle to needle, some of the strands so loose they nearly touched the land while others were so tight they were many thousands of miles up in the sky. Creatures great and greater made their nests on the bridges but none seemed to be aware that anything out of the ordinary was about to occur over their heads.

Whing had lost his wig while hanging from the side of the steeple as he hung now, had it fall from the little round knob back of his brow and drift away into the clouds. He took it from the head of a snape who somehow got onto one of the high bridges, and he missed the thing. For some reason he had felt more intelligent when wearing it.

There were no clouds obstructing his view at the moment and he could look down at an ocean. It looked like a little piece of slate.

Back up the side rail he went to find admission into the laboratory through one of the vent tunnels. On his way he

passed Odeeda but didn't wave or speak to her because he
wasn't in the mood for a domestic battle. She would soon give
birth to his child and it wasn't his intent that she become
nervous or upset, at least not until the important moment. Then
he would behave with her according to her performance.

The ship was a long cylinder from a planet called Laredo.
All spacecraft were constructed in the same manner so that
they would be able to dock in the tops of the steeples. Now
the vehicle edged slowly down into the yawning mouth, blasting stardrive matter thousands of miles in every direction. Too
high up to harm the planet, the material scattered on the solar
wind and eventually dissipated light-years away.

With anxious anticipation Whing observed the monitoring
screen inside the lab and waited for the spacemen to emerge
from the lock into the pressurized confines of the steeple house.
He considered it strange that the process was taking so long.
There the lock was opening at last, and a pair of funny little
objects moved from the ship into the corridor leading to the
living quarters, but there were no men anywhere to be seen.
As the lock suddenly closed, Whing experienced a stab of raw
grief. He was lonely for his own kind, not the creatures living
on the bridges between steeples but for those who plied the
starpaths. Here one of the machines had docked in the maw
but the pilot and his crew weren't being hasty enough about
making themselves visible. Whing wondered how long they
would remain in their machine. When were they going to come
out?

For the sake of curiosity he clambered into a tunnel that led
into the living rooms and began picking his way along the
slippery steel flooring. His movements alerted the two little
stalks, who resembled pink and brown worms now that they
had removed their outer skin and were naked. Whing was
astonished that they were living creatures. Perhaps they were
a necessary part of the ship's complement, mechanics or some
such, or they could be servants of the men. On second thought,
they were probably entertainers.

All this was conjecture while the plain reality was that the
worms displayed hostile reactions upon sight of the sentry
coming through the large vent in their living room. All he had

in mind at the moment was to find out if they were intelligent enough to communicate. Then he smelled them and realized how hungry he was.

One of the worms made him a small meal while the other ran into an elevator. Rather than chase the thing, Whing went back to the lab to watch the monitoring screen. Sooner or later the spacemen were bound to emerge from the ship.

He believed he was a man. In truth, he was a steeple sentry, not one of a kind but rare enough so that anyone coming onto the planet wouldn't be anticipating him. He had evolved in the nooks and crannies of the skyscraper embedded in the Earth's surface and jutting miles into space. His evolution had been rapid because the seepage from the chemical dump found its way into those same nooks and crannies. It was possible that one of his ancestors had been a mite or a beetle or some other leggy thing.

Somewhere along the way the lineage that eventually produced him lost its wings. The ultimate offspring of that lineage was too heavy to fly, but he could move like lightning in or out of the steeple parts. He was impervious to atmosphere or vacuum and possessed a brain pan that wasn't exactly stuffed to the brim.

At times when provisions were low and nothing came clambering across the strands at lower levels he had a tidbit or two from the cadaver depository, or he snacked on tubes and vials in the research lab. One day he butted a gleaming cabinet that broke into shards and buried a piece of material in his brain. Odd coincidence drove it through one of the few penetrable points on his head. Clinging to the sliver were some frozen memory cells extracted from a long dead human and preserved in the cabinet for futurity. For a while the pierced part of Whing's brain was comatose but then it revived and absorbed the living cells. That was when he began thinking he was a man. His knowledge was sketchy because individual cells didn't hold much information and he had been inflicted with only a few.

A vermin came snooping about outside the five-foot-thick window, banged on it until Whing finally gave up waiting for the men to come out of the ship. The airlock he always used was large; otherwise he would have kicked down the walls, thereby rendering the compartment useless to legitimate astronauts. By the time he reached the outside, the vermin had run away. He could see it climbing down the girders below him but only for a moment or two did he consider giving chase. It was time for him to go home.

Odeeda had given birth. So disgusted was he that she hadn't born a live child but only dropped a stupid egg that he kicked her out of the nest and all the way off the bridge. She fell several miles, fortunately landing on another set of strands. By the time she climbed back to her egg, Whing's temper had dissipated and he was willing to make up with her. He was certain there was a live manchild of his somewhere in their future.

No more eggs, he warned her and then later he was angered anew when she tried to eat him. Somewhere back in her genealogy a particularly virulent individual had been so nearsighted that when her mate retreated in her nest to rest and then made a few innocent movements she mistook him for an edible stranger. Now Whing had to beat Odeeda on the back of the head with his fists so she would recognize him and leave off trying to destroy him.

He went back up to the lab and the monitoring screen to watch for the spacemen to come out of the craft. While resting and observing, he heard a noise in another part of the area, climbed into the vent and retraced his steps of several hours before. The brown worm who escaped into the elevator earlier had sneaked back inside, donned his strange clothing and was now attempting to get to the ship.

There wasn't time for him to reach the airlock in the docking compound before Whing emerged from the vent, so he ran back into the elevator. Whing was annoyed enough to go outside and climb down a girder alongside the machine. He could see into the compartment through a window and the more intently he stared at the puny creature the more he came to realize that it had a head and a face, the latter being extremely unattractive and even silly looking. But the whole worm was tasty and it was worth it for the steeple sentry to speed down the girders and keep pace with the el. There was always the chance that the creature would come out and join him.

All of a sudden the machine changed direction and went back up toward the vacuum of outer space. Whing wasn't inconvenienced, being agile and strong. He began climbing upward once again. Inside the elevator the worm cringed and even seemed to swoon for a while, lay down on the floor of the cage and was quite motionless for several hours. Since Whing slept while he was awake, he didn't know what the worm was doing. Instead of having a monitor that shut down an entire section of his brain every so often, he blinked on and off all the time like a light. He was asleep one moment and awake the next moment and then asleep, et cetera. Consequently he was never tired or invigorated but rather steamed along at a pace sufficiently active for his life-style; or his life-style was determined by the fact that physical extremes were foreign to him. He could climb a thousand miles of steeple rails in a few minutes so he didn't consider that his was a shuffling species. However he didn't have a great many comparisons available since he was unsociable and hadn't much to do with anyone other than Odeeda.

During the time he was lost in reverie concerning the finer qualities of himself and his ancestors, the worm rode skyward in still another attempt to get to the ship. The sentry knew the stranger's intent and stationed himself between the top of the el and the docking platform. Driven by hunger and perhaps other incentives, the worm forsook the elevator and ran through the living quarters to the frozen food cupboards. Gathering up an armful of items he raced back to the el and was safely on his journey downward before Whing could get through the lock.

Down the outside girders the large individual climbed at what seemed to him a slow pace. Through the window he spied on the worm who seemed to be doing the same thing to him. After staring for a time at the little ball atop the creature, the steeple sentry could begin making out facial features of a sort. The foreigner had on his artificial suit but inside he was a brown body with four appendages, long yellow hair and brown eyes. A revolting little piece of life he was and Whing longed to know why he existed and what he was about. His longing wasn't intense, when he thought about it. Worms weren't essential in the schemes of the universe, and this one would terminate in the belly of a denizen in the reaches below.

Now and then the worm ate and occasionally lay down in a swoon, and all the while the machine slid rapidly and silently toward the planet's surface.

It didn't take more than a day or two for Whing to decide to leave the being in the elevator to its fate and returned to the dizzy heights of the steeple. The air below made him feel stifled and clumsy. Though he could survive there and he would infrequently take a vacation on one of the lower strands, still, it wasn't his favorite environment, being too crowded with foliage and overpopulated with creatures who had more belligerence than sense. Most of the lowlife hadn't the intelligence to avoid the big blue sentry, with his nearly invulnerable hide and at least a portion of a man's brain.

At his leisure, Whing climbed back up the spires that had always been his home. The closer he approached the topmost part of the maw the better he felt, until at last he stood on a section of the opening into which the spaceship had inched. It was there now, about a hundred and fifty miles lower, sitting and throbbing like a heart, with its computers thinking and its motors waiting for someone to give them a command. Somewhere inside were surely large blue spacemen who would make an appearance and be amazed when their humble relative revealed himself to them.

In a kind of salute he extended a horny finger toward the blazing lamp that was the sun. Streamers played out from its edges, tugged and strained as if they were being held captive by what looked like a solid rim. Now and then there was a belching movement that sent gobs of flame hurtling away into dark reaches.

The sentry felt a touch of loneliness as he stared at the void. What he needed was the scalp he had taken from the snape. It had made him feel good but it was gone now, having fallen down through the clouds. To retrieve it he must make the long trip to the lower strands or perhaps even all the way to the ground. With a sigh, he looked back at the splashing sun. It wasn't worth going after; it wouldn't be there when he arrived. Only up here was reality changeless. Down there it was a mad jungle.

Chapter 2

Pip knew as soon as he put on the hairy little wig Kadooka gave him that this was going to be the best scam he had ever pulled. The thing fit over the top of his skull and seemed to grow invisible fingers that went down inside his head to play with certain parts of his brain. They were his pleasure centers, without a doubt, and even as he realized what was happening he wasn't disturbed. His brain wasn't so holy that it couldn't be messed with, even if permission was yet to be gained. In other words the pleasure the wig gave him felt so good that he didn't care about anything.

The jolts or rushes weren't so steady, intense or even frequent that he was immediately worn out, but in fact it took an entire day before he grew weary. It seemed fine to him. This way he could enjoy his fun and sleep at night. What could be better? He knew in a cloudy kind of way that the hat wasn't a hat or wig at all but was a part of some creature that was now or had once been alive. It would be necessary for him to test it, try it out for a week or so, to discover its side effects. Hopefully it would have none. In the meantime the scam must go on. Big Kadooka must be gotten rid of. He must be lulled, his suspicions had to be put to rest, after which Pip intended to sneak away with the merchandise. Fraud was his profession and suckers his bread and butter, though he had never heard of such items.

"The ornad will be a fierce antagonist," said Kadooka.

"Not to worry."

13

"That's easy for you to say while you're wearing the hat. Maybe you ought to remove it until after the job is done. It could fog your judgment."

"Who's afraid of an old ornad?" said Pip, wondering what an ornad was. Probably one of those leaping uglies that lived on the bridges. He stood on a fat leaf growing from the trunk of an old tree whose beginning or end he couldn't see. All that came into view was heavy jungle, green and damp with dew, while through a vast fern overhead peeped a patch of blue sky.

Slightly to his right and above him sat Kadooka on a limb, a large and lumbering man who made no threats with his mouth but a myriad of them with his expression and gestures. Now he squatted and leaned down to stare at the youth, who agreed to relieve him of the wig in exchange for the ornad's disposal. The youth sold insurance, so he claimed. For payment he slew other people's enemies. Kadooka's opinions about such claims remained a mystery, as he was a brooding, scowling sort who looked as if he might prefer action to conversation; hostile action.

Kadooka had two pretty sisters named DeLoona and LaLa. The latter had told Pip with her eyes that if he wanted to come courting she wouldn't be disagreeable.

He didn't intend to court or even hang around because though he didn't know what an ornad was he firmly believed in its existence. The proof positive of that fact lay on his head making his reality sublime. Perhaps too sublime. Usually he took payment in exotic foods, jewelry, fine clothing or similar items. Never before had he been offered an hallucinogen.

"It feels good, doesn't it?" said Kadooka.

"I think I'll go hunt for that old ornad."

"He isn't that way. I told you he was northeast, about a mile. Every once in a while he comes tearing into camp, and if you don't do your job I might be forced to consider moving. I don't intend doing that unless I have to and if I have to I'll be mad."

"I remember the direction. Don't worry about my memory. You don't expect me to approach him via a direct route, do you?"

Kadooka gave a nasty grin and leaned farther from the limb.

He was brutish in appearance with only a piece of plantskin covering his middle. Pip had never seen so much chest hair on a man. "I don't expect you to approach him from any route at all," said Kadooka. "I think you're trying to pull a fast one on me and I'm looking forward to beating your brains out. Insurance salesman, eh? What did you ever kill, twerp?"

Looking offended, Pip said, "Why did you give me the wig if you have no faith in me?"

"I'm willing to take drastic measures even when the chances are so slim. Northeast, kid, and don't think I'm letting you out of my sight for a second."

Not disheartened in the least, Pip dropped from the leaf onto a thin limb that extended more than a mile through the dense foliage. In his experience people were generally like Kadooka, suspicious, disbelieving and quick to threaten, but they always relinquished their valuables in hopes that the fresh-faced newcomer would slice away their troubles with his keen confidence. Their suspicions remained at the fore, though, and they tried to follow the slim and agile salesman to the battleground. They always lost him in the green while he made tracks toward distant destinations with their wealth tied to his belt, or slapped on his head, in this case.

It went well for the time being, the events occurring as he anticipated until he realized that this time an essential ingredient was missing. This time he couldn't lose his shadow or, in other words, Kadooka wasn't falling behind. The course hadn't been easy. Though not familiar with this particular tree, Pip chose the most difficult byways, the narrowest passages, the sheerest climbs.

A con man almost by virtue of his genes, he had never seen the day he couldn't outrun someone as big as the man behind him, so he began climbing the tree faster than he ordinarily would. From one limb to another he swung and clambered, finally stopping to rest. Then he took a look behind him. He had done it, managed to outdistance the hairy hulk who was too cowardly to dispose of his ornad himself.

Pip breathed deeply of the sweet air and took the time to hit the tree limb with the side of his sword, thus discouraging a young snape in the act of climbing onto the perch. The creature pretended to be intent upon searching for parasites on its belly. It was furry and single of eye with four thin arms and two legs. After giving Pip several furtive glances, it climbed down to lower levels where small food could be found.

The air was damp and redolent and suited Pip just fine. His body absorbed moisture but not so much that he became too heavy to be active. At the first sign of rain he would immediately take shelter and not even Kadooka could pry him from concealment. Not that Kadooka liked too much rain either. Already he was gross without having soaked up a deal of water.

For some reason there were a great many braided vines on both sides of the tree limb along which Pip hurried. They looked peculiar, almost as if an intelligent hand had fashioned them, but that had to be impossible. Whoever heard of people entwining vines? Never had he seen so many braids and he didn't like them because they were barriers that prevented him from taking an alternate route. This limb led straight out to a bridge and he wanted to get off it as quickly as possible.

He stopped where he was and began to perspire. What was it about those braided fences? Cocking his head to listen, he heard snapes, budgers, frallops, cremonts and all the other jungle fauna, but he didn't hear any birds. Nor did he see any of those winged specimens, which meant they had all gone into hiding. On a day like this there ought to be flocks of them winging over and under the bridge and through the foliage, or at least they should be making noises in their nests.

Slowly he backed up. Not looking behind him, he cautiously retraced his steps along the limb. To his consternation his movements were inhibited by a laced fabric made of reeds and vines. Kadooka had crept up and tied another braided fence to the foliage so that it was impossible for Pip to get off the limb. It seemed he was in a closed corridor with only one way out.

The youth's sweat ran in rivulets down his neck. Kadooka was a menace to a healthy young con man, especially one who desired to remain that way. All was at peace in the world save for one nervous insurance salesman who didn't care how the wig on his head played with his pleasure centers. He was still scared. Hastily he removed the furry covering and stuck it in his belt.

"I can't work under these conditions," he said in a loud voice to the jumble of flora beyond the rear screen. No one responded to his words. "I'm as courageous as the next man but how do you think I feel being caged this way?" There was no reply from Kadooka. "If you keep hedging up my way I'll have to cancel your insurance," he said.

The limb beneath his sticky feet trembled. The sweat from his body had mingled with tree sap and now he couldn't walk as rapidly as he wished. Not that there was any way to go except farther out on the limb where the trembling seemed more vigorous.

"I quit!" he said to the jungle. Where was Kadooka? "Hey, have you gone?" he yelled. Was he enraged or terrified? Why was the limb bucking under him and why had the traitor hemmed him in and then run away? Did he already know the answers to his questions?

Without asking for it or anticipating it, he had been duped. For the first time in his brief career he had met a sucker who hadn't swallowed his practiced line. Instead of being permitted to play out a little fraud, he was going to be forced to perform the duty for which he had been paid.

In a frallop's eye! First he climbed the fences to the sides and then he climbed the one behind him and overhead. There wasn't anything underneath save for an empty space so sheer he didn't want to look. In no way could he survive the fall if he left the limb.

With an unsteady step he walked forward to meet his fate, his sword in his hand, his eyes darting in every direction in search of a way out. In disgust he looked at his weapon. Made of a bird's upper bill, it was sharp enough but he owned it primarily to peel fruit and to skin game, certainly not to kill ornads or anything else.

He approached the matter at hand with no curiosity. And then he saw it. An ornad turned out to be a hellion. That meant it was large, dangerous and full of hostility toward anything and everything. It lived on the strands and in fact helped string the bridge that dangled between two steeples. Omnivorous, it liked to drag its meal out onto its nest, devour all but the bones unless they happened to be soft, and decorate its home with them. The nest smelled to high heaven and presented a grisly sight to the timid man who poked his head from the foliage to see what Kadooka expected him to combat.

If the situation hadn't been so fraught with menace it might have been amusing. The sound he made when he first glimpsed the creature wasn't at all like a laugh but was more a scream. Never had he deliberately done anything to hurt anyone and here he was being treated like a gangster.

The ornad heard the cry, gave off exploring the inside of a skull with its tongue and turned to stare at the tree a quarter-mile away. It plainly had keen hearing. Now and then a portion of it sagged onto the particular string running directly through the part of the tree where Pip crouched and stared.

The monster was green and yellow, beautifully reticulated, if one cared for that sort of artistry. Hound-dog ears adorned the sides of the long head, large and green like bundy leaves and capable of standing straight up in the air whenever the beast grew alert. He had sixteen legs and a stingered tail but his most formidable weapons were his teeth. He somewhat resembled a caterpillar of old, blown thousands of times to a size greater than the original.

Alarmed and sweaty but not yet panicked, Pip hid in the tree and looked in awe at the grisly character doing away with the carcass of a full-grown budger. The nest was large and oval in shape, made of vines, tree limbs, straw, moss, reeds and the bones from past meals. In the center of it lay the ornad, sucking the skull, occasionally glaring at the tree, once in a while coiling its long body and then dropping its rear end onto the strand running through the thickest part of Pip's sanctuary.

Kadooka had to be crazy to think anyone in his right mind or out of it would face the titan out there on the nest! Crazy or evil! Dry of mouth, Pip began again to inch backward along the limb. With an oath he realized that the traitor had dropped another fence behind him! While he wasn't paying attention Kadooka cut away the rear fence, crept near to the youth and set up another barrier. Now Pip was stuck on the end of the limb, wondering what kind of man it was who could handle vines inches in diameter as if they were tiny grass blades.

No matter, there had to be an escape route. Always there had been one and this time would be no different.

The ornad was in a bad mood. Perhaps the budger hadn't satisfied his hunger. In a rage he flung the skull into the emptiness on every side of him. It fell two thousand feet into a hidden lake.

It had never happened this way before. Always Pip was able to slip away from danger or outrun the victims of his scams. There had been plenty of times when indignant suckers took to his trail but no matter how intense their dedication they eventually gave up. People had a tendency to grow soft and lazy in their middle years and they were usually the target of Pip's interest. The fact was he had never been near peril. It was easy to avoid if one was intelligent and alert. Now he crouched and felt of the trail behind him without taking his eyes off the horrendous ornad who sat on its nest flinging bones at the sky.

His probing fingers touched the limb behind him and then he touched something soft and furry. There was a large snape sitting looking at him while the sun gleamed off its teeth. Kadooka had been doubly treacherous, removed the rear fence and prodded the beast into the enclosure.

Pip would have been better off had he remained silent. Possibly the snape might have blundered out onto the strands in an attempt to get away, he could have been seen and apprehended by the ornad and during the activity Pip could quietly sneak away. It didn't happen that way. The snape was an adult with big teeth, and its single eye wasn't the normal dark color. It was light blue, almost white. Added to that, another curiosity made him more menacing. He had no scalp, only a scarred dome that looked like a wrinkled face. The sum of his unattractiveness caused Pip to leap backward and cry out.

He landed on the strands, left the limb altogether and fell on the smelly strings of material fashioned by the uglies who lived high above the world. The snape considered the situation and his alternatives and packed it in by clambering across the man and climbing hand over hand along the underside of the limb. There were plenty of knots and bumps to afford him all the holds he needed. The last Pip saw of him he was swinging down to safety and invisibility.

Alerted, the ornad sat balanced on his lower end with the rest of him poking several feet into the air. His ears were pointed straight up and his hideous eyes had already spied Pip sprawled on his front path. With an ear-splitting shriek he prepared for battle by wrapping his lower body around a sagging strand. Clouds of dust arose while half a ton of debris fell in bits and pieces all the way to the ground.

There was time for Pip to think about getting up and following the snape. He didn't have the climbing ability of the limber creature but at times such as this he possessed unlimited energy. That was all the time there was, though, and he couldn't make a plan to save himself. The maniacal ornad wasn't running across the bridge toward him as he had anticipated but instead whizzed through space while clinging to a dangling strand. It would be upon him in a matter of seconds. Its little feet reached for him and so did its toothy mouth. It didn't hang down headfirst. The powerful muscles in its lengthy torso allowed it to hold onto the strand and stand up almost upright. In fact it needn't have coiled its rear around the string but could have gripped with its many feet. But then it couldn't take the victim in its teeth right away. It would have to let go its support and it plainly didn't want to do that.

Panting in terror, Pip watched the monster speed his way. He stood on a thick string just short of the tree limb. He hadn't many choices. Certain that he was about to die, he thought of jumping out into space. His fumbling fingers touched his sword, picked it up from where it had fallen, and then he crouched and hacked at the strands.

The cutting edge was sharp and he was lucky. The strand supporting the ornad gave way just as the animal was about to reach for its target. As the green killer fell away into emptiness one of its claws raked Pip's face. The man fell unconscious onto the bridge while the ornad swung back the other way, down and ever downward for many yards, until the string ran out and he collided with a tree stump growing on a hillside on the ground.

Chapter 3

Ferrer Burgoyne thought he was on the ground. It didn't occur to him that a machine would malfunction at such an important and hazardous moment in his career. In reality the elevator was temporarily jammed by a nest something had built in a corner of one of the girders. Little by little the debris seeped inside and became a tough wad that slowed the vehicle and made Ferrer believe he had arrived at his destination.

Some destination. Seen from the sky the planet didn't look so forbidding, being vividly green and soft in appearance. Like a lovely lap; the bosom of nature; the birthplace of his forefathers; home. As soon as he stepped out onto what he thought was solid ground, the elevator door shut and continued on down without him. At true ground level it would begin the long trip back up to the ship, empty and uninhabited, without him. He wanted nothing more to do with it. Another confrontation with the blue monster in the sky and he would have to commit suicide. Better that than insanity.

He wanted to weep or at least sniffle. He wore a spacesuit that caused him to swelter as soon as he stepped into the hotbox of Earth. Onto the hotbox; beneath terrible, malodorous strands of vegetation where carbon dioxide, oxygen, heat and fear were perpetually captured. It was the heat that made him perspire, not the suit, or perhaps it was his imagination. It was a good suit, not really constructed to keep him cool in an inferno but rather to keep him warm in a vacuum.

He blew against his visor and laughed. Who was he kidding?

21

He could never go back up to the ship because Satan in the form of a multi-legged hellion sat up there waiting for him. It had already killed Carpall, crunched and munched him like Crackerjacks and it would love to add little Ferrer to the junk in its stomach.

He felt little. He also felt stupid, unlucky, persecuted, hated and victimized. What else could he do but locate the signal station somewhere down there on the ground? During the attempt he would probably be snatched by one of the predators dotting the upper and lower landscapes of this loathsome place.

With loving hands he stripped off the suit and stuffed it into the strands so that it couldn't be seen. He had changed his mind. If it was the last thing he did, he would come back for it and go up there and face that blue hellion again. One of these days. If he could. Never mind how dumb the idea was. All he needed to do was get into the ship or into the communication station in the steeple.

All at once he felt like smacking himself in the forehead. He could have tried the communications station while he was up there but he hadn't even thought about it. Paramount in his mind had been the need to get lower and away from the creature. Why had he even left the el at all? He didn't know; or rather he did know. Scared out of his wits he had behaved witlessly.

Wondering how far he was from the ground he stepped across the strands and looked down. Immediately stricken with vertigo, he staggered backward. All he could see down there was a gray cloud speeding toward him like an ocean. Any minute he expected it to break over him and carry him to his death.

Naked, perspiring, he began walking across the bridge. He might as well, having nowhere else to go and being unable to climb down the steeple. The girders were too large to be handled by anything but giant monsters.

The strands had been built to support huge creatures, so he had no trouble finding solid footing. As he walked he marveled at the strings. Some of them were feet or inches in diameter while others were millimeters thick. Who or what had built the first bridges between steeples? Birds. That's what they said.

That's what they had told him. Ordinary birds. What bird could carry one of these fat threads?

What about the blue monster at the top of the steeple? Reports indicated that undesirable but minor mutations had occurred on Earth, for what reasons no one was really sure. The reports themselves were vague, too sketchy, and as a matter of fact very little information was available from any source. What of the blue monster? Ferrer Burgoyne and his co-astronaut had never dreamed such a horror existed. To be certain they were aware that mutations were on the planet, which was why Project Deep Green had been put into the works in the first place. Ferrer and Carpall were supposed to have used a small flying craft to make a map of the immediate vicinity. Later they would have come back from Laredo and drawn another map of the terrain around another steeple. Their mission had been peaceful, although they didn't comprehend the end results of their labor. Not exactly.

Ferrer was sick almost unto death with his fear and his hatred of this world. It was like a grisly spawn of itself, hostile and inhospitable to its own offspring. Step by step he moved out onto a no-man's land two thousand feet above a body of water that had eaten away at a continent for billions of years.

It didn't matter to him how ancient Earth was. He had never been particularly fond of old things anyhow, except that he loved Laredo which was much older than this place. There was a scratch on the brown skin of his belly, grass in his long yellow hair and a pain in his gut. He didn't want to be Earthy.

By and by the bridge began to sway and he realized he was approaching some foul and cumbersome entity moving around and around on a patch of strands like a dog getting ready to lie down. This entity had the ears of a dog but it was no canine. Or, to be more accurate, it had a single hound-dog-like appendage, the other having been sheared off when the ornad collided with the stump after its meeting with Pip. Bruised, battered but a stranger to remorse, it prepared to settle down for a recuperative period. From the corner of one eye it saw Ferrer but considered him to be no more than a reed swaying in the wind.

Disgorging the last meal he had eaten in the elevator, Ferrer

crouched and cursed his thundering heart. What was this mad
vision his traumatized imagination concocted? The ornad
looked somewhat like a gigantic green and yellow caterpillar,
having a body made of nimble sections. The head was also
similar to that tiny life of the past, being snouty and round or
slanted near the brow, but there were no ineffectual little feet
on this creature. He had sixteen green legs with long toes and
thumbs on his feet or hands. As for his teeth, they were sharp
and prominent. Now he laid his bloody head on his nest and
groaned in pain and rage. Once in a while he looked up to see
what had become of the walking reed of brown and yellow
colors.

His sensibilities offended by everything that had happened
to him thus far, Ferrer tramped nearer to the hideous beast and
then began walking on tiptoe. Somewhere a whirlwind was
born, came to buffet him, tried to fling him away. He buried
his feet in tangled vines and cursed aloud. Behind him were
miles of strands and the jutting steeple while ahead was what
looked like a forest. Between both was the ornad who had
decided to try to sleep away his discomfort.

Stepping to the edge of the bridge Ferrer leaned down and
hunted until he found what he was looking for, a solid under-
bridge or some pathway on the underside of the span that he
could use to sneak past the creature. At this point he was
reckless almost to the point of insanity. When in the midst of
hell, why search for the angelic? Such was his rationalization
to himself.

The air on the bridge had become extremely redolent since
he was fairly near to the creature's nest and the various remains
of meals. The smell heightened his sense of indignation and
he readily swung over the side, found a foothold, positioned
himself securely and crept forward along narrow strings. Even
the loose ones were wide enough to support him though most
of the time he had to give up walking and crawled because
they didn't hang down far enough.

Some movement or bodily sound he made intruded upon
the ornad's consciousness. He was directly beneath the nest
when the beast poked its head over the edge to see what was
happening. Ferrer shrieked but managed to maintain his bal-

ance, even when the ornad came partially into his territory under the bridge. Its front feet probed for him as did the dripping fangs but he moved sideways so that the beast momentarily raised up and tried reaching for him from another direction. Meanwhile he continued moving ahead, and it abandoned its ploy and moved along with him. Debris slipped through the cracks between strands and rained on him like the shredded contents of many coffins.

Choking and cursing, now and then giving voice to a frantic bellow, he crawled and scrambled toward the tree. He didn't dare look up for fear he would spy a green hand coming through or around after him, and he was afraid to look down because the loose strings were growing farther apart. There were a hundred ways in which the strands ran through and outside the large tree. Some disappeared below the clouds while others missed the growth altogether and reached into the fog toward another steeple many miles distant.

In desperation Ferrer heaved himself free of the confining strands, dangled toward the faraway lake and painstakingly began working his way toward a limb. Hand over hand he went, gasping and still cursing, confident that the strands would hold so that he could survive and be subjected to more torture and horrifying visions in the foliage beyond.

The ornad realized what his prey was attempting to do and moved his great carcass as rapidly as he could. He was even tempted to try a jungle swing but then recalled what happened the last time he tried it. Not wishing to lose his other ear, he remained on top of the bridge and hoped to arrive in the tree before the worm.

He was too large and the tree limbs were too flimsy. The brown one swung hand over hand to the first green protuberance, grasped a handful of leaves and pulled himself from the span. The last the ornad saw of him was his skinned behind fading into the leaves. The creature could have followed him. Often he climbed into the tree and roamed about, marauding and terrifying the natives, but the confines were tight and today he had a sore head. Besides he wasn't really hungry. With a sigh of relief he turned and lumbered back to his nest.

Calming down a bit and satisfied that his heart wasn't going to burst through his chest just then, Ferrer slowly traversed the limb. He marveled that he still wasn't chilled though he was now in deep shade. Standing with his hand gently clutching an overhead leaf, he stood staring about him at the most verdant spot he had ever seen or imagined. The scenes in antique Tarzan films that he had viewed in his anthropology classes were nothing like this, and not just because those old films were in black and white. Nowhere had there been trees this size with limbs, mere limbs, ten and twenty feet in diameter. Nor did those ancient reels show fruit as big as baskets. It was more than just what he saw. Every sense that he owned was being bombarded with a single stimulus and he finally realized what it was. Life.

As for the colors, he closed his eyes because his body was beginning to feel like a sponge soaking up too much sweetness. Cautiously he opened them. He stood still not knowing which way to go when all of a sudden a lilting tune came to him from an unseen source, piercing the raucous cacophony of birds and other fauna. It sounded like a radio and he thought for a moment that the heat had finally gotten to him and he was hallucinating. Then the sound came again, soft and delicate, like tiny tappings against fragile chimes, low at first and then tripping up the scale of notes to a quick clustering that sounded like laughter.

Full of curiosity he stepped toward a lavender-colored flower, stuck his ear nearer to it and listened. From the deep opening came a few musical notes. The plant was singing. Most of it was green but its blossoms at the end of long stems were vivid enough, ranging in shade from deep purple on the edges of the petals and gradually becoming white. They were like open bells and inside them were writhing tips or fingers that seemed to be beckoning to him. Captivated by wonder he stepped closer and moved to cup one of the bells in his hand. He wanted to touch it, smell it, examine. It suddenly opened wide and darted forward to slap itself flat against his arm. He didn't feel anything but he couldn't pull away from the blossom.

All at once he stopped and stared at something behind the plant. Straight ahead and looking out at him from between two huge green leaves were two eyes in a face.

His lower jaw dropped while his own eyes went round. What he was seeing had to be impossible. There were no people on Earth nor had there been for thousands of years. The last men to travel to the stars had been the . . . last . . . men.

This specimen stepped onto the limb and stood regarding him with interest. It was taller by a head than he but was about the same weight. The hair was short, curly and black, the face was round like the moon, the eyes were small and lacking any white, just green, like marble with light shining through. The skin was smooth and almost shiny as if it were stretched taut or as if it were simply different.

Ferrer's second thought was that the creature wasn't human, could never be human. Again he remembered that Earth held none of his species. Since birth or shortly thereafter he had been taught as much.

"Hello," he said.

The person came forward, one foot in front of the other as any person would walk and then Ferrer became aware of the stranger's clothing. It wore an almost transparent garment, like onion skin, from waist to knee. As for the torso, it seemed familiar enough, what with jutting ribs and collarbones, but where each flat breast should have been was a small round globe. Ferrer felt insane. Not only were there things on the planet that looked like men, there were also things that resembled women.

His breath suddenly began coming in gasps. Waves of horror swept over him as he felt the strength of his beliefs washing out of him. It wasn't that he was afraid of women. He feared no woman or man as long as they fit into the preconceived notions set up in his mind by several generations of Laredo ancestors.

This woman frightened him nearly to death. She had all the fixtures of a human being but something was terribly out of focus. Perhaps it was her skin. Yes, that was probably it. She was green like the pulp of an unripe honeydew melon; not dark green at all; a little bit green; a light tinge; almost human but not at all pink or brown as humans should be.

Wondering if he was staring straight into the face of a walking plant, Ferrer swayed on the limb. He felt as if he were behaving badly but he couldn't help it. No matter what he faced he ought to have the courage of a civilized man.

"Careful or you'll fall," DeLoona said in the clicking, slurred speech of her kind. Plainly the brown one didn't understand her. Tone, though, counted more than words. "Are you all right? Can I help you in any way?"

A walking, talking plant that looked like a woman. Ferrer was near enough to smell her perspiration. She smiled at him with teeth the color of a dowager's hair, so white with that faint hint of blue. Why weren't they green? Walking, talking, sweat that reminded him of the smell of sassafras, green eyes, blue teeth, two breasts like his mother, it was too much, too clashing, too unexpected for him to absorb. Earth had no right to support mutations. It belonged to him and his kind.

She shocked him even further. Raising a wicked-looking weapon that looked like a piece of bone, she whacked the flower off his arm, sliced it away along with a layer of his flesh.

"You shouldn't have gotten so close to the siren," she said. "It would have eaten you, you know. Don't you know? Really, you're the strangest stranger I've ever met."

There was a loud buzzing in Ferrer's ears. The last hours had been too much for him and then there was the added trauma that his arm pained him terribly while his blood ran down onto his feet.

As far as he was concerned he pitched out into empty space in a dead swoon. As far as DeLoona was concerned the brown man fainted in her arms.

Chapter 4

Peru acquired his formal name by virtue of the fact that his first host or discoverer had a speech defect. It came from the letters P.U. which the host repeated every once in a while after he stumbled into the old cave and picked up the infection.

Having lain dormant since no one knew when, Peru wasn't grateful to be carried from the dark cave into the light of day. He hadn't the sense to know the difference. If one were to describe his inner and outer package one might have said he was an ugly little microbe.

Following the dictates of his nature he worked his way into the shoulder of his host who had brushed against a nasty spot sticking to the wall of the cave. From there the germ sought daylight by boring through the man's body.

There was little intelligence in the human for he had been dropped on his head in infancy, but he knew a bad smell when one confronted him, and so whenever the odor from the suppurating sore on his chest wafted upward he said, "P. U." The sound of the utterance resounded inside the scant corporeal makeup of Disease which later decided to take it for his name, or one of them. Before he was through he would be called many things, mostly disparaging.

Peru had feelings of nostalgia whenever he thought of the two noises comprising his title, a sensation of homesickness and a longing to return to the nest, though he forgot where or what the nest had been. Had he recalled the characteristics of his original host he would have been filled with anger and

29

disgust. At any rate, his affinity for his nomenclature might well have been his sole claim to good, as opposed to evil or as opposed to whatever the other life forms around him wanted or did. He wasn't like any of them and indeed, in an abstract way of thinking, he was an absolute antithesis to them and their existence. He was non-direct, non-forward, not backward. He was *nothing*. Being annoyed him, not his own but that of reality. He hated things, sights and realizations. As he matured he dedicated himself to ridding the world of them and detected no contradiction in the concepts.

After he killed that first man he lay in the corpse under some tall grass until a chicken came by and stepped in the putrefying mass. The bird carried Infection away on his feet and went about his business until his legs rotted off, at which time he fell down and died.

Meanwhile Peru ate the chicken's head and brain. The inferior memory cells were stored in his body until he acquired a rudimentary intellect. If he walked about he would find food. There were dangers and sensations that weren't unpleasant but he needn't waste time worrying about disaster because life was brief anyway. So thought the chicken while he was alive and so thought Peru later. In addition there was virulence, greed and an unspoken and unrealized longing to play havoc, to seep, consume, stink, befoul and utterly ruin. These qualities were innate in the murderous infection so he didn't have to pick them up from any of his victims.

It was also innate in the tiny criminal to wish to travel in a benevolent disguise, therefore had anyone told him he looked like a globule of bloody pus he would have been offended. Having the intelligence of a chicken he didn't know what he looked like but secretly he realized how much more rewarding his days would be were he to appeal to the better nature of his victims and not the worst. Thus, after his intelligence grew, he tried to be fastidious in speech, appearance and manner, except of course when he stooped to doing what he liked best which was to make a mess of everything and everyone around him. Save for a few subconscious wishes to die before he matured, his view of himself and his mission was sanguine.

One day a man from a tribe of woman-haters came through

the upper forest in search of the wife he had stashed away in a cavern of ivy. It bereaved him to discover that some filthy kind of disease had gotten to her while he was gone and now she sat swooning against a limb while an infection gorged on the side of her face.

The woman had picked Peru up on a stick, held him higher to get a good look at him and then couldn't get out of the way quickly enough when he dropped onto an open sore on her face. Her husband tried treating her but she was plainly going to die and was suffering a great deal so he mercifully shoved his sword into her heart. Then in a rage because he loved her he cut off her head and set fire to it in hopes of getting revenge on the disease. Unwittingly he had rammed his sword into the wound and carried Peru's essence away with him to his camp. On the way home he cleaned his weapon on his thigh and accidentally gave himself a minor slice.

This time infection wasn't so obvious and afflicted his host in secretive places so that the man's companions couldn't account for his behavior. He had fits and experienced inexplicable rages and eventually they isolated him in one of the innumerable ivy caves and carried food and water to him.

"I have a wife, you know," he said to the guard who was seldom away from his duty.

"How can you say such a thing? We're dedicated to non-reproduction!"

"Maybe so, but I still have a wife, or I had one until that thing killed her. Spread the word in case someone gets an idea about how to combat it. I don't think it's a common ordinary infection or disease. If I didn't know better I'd say it was intelligent. Tell the others to be careful and not let it near a cut in the skin. I think it's . . . I don't know what it is but I figure I didn't kill it. I thought I did but the bugger's in my gut playing games."

"Don't tell anybody about what you said," said the guard.

"You mean about my wife? Why not? You have one, too."

"Of course I have nothing of the kind!"

Peru's host groaned and suffered. "We should have named ourselves the society of hypocrites. Hate women? That's easy to do until you reach puberty."

"That's only nature's way of beguiling you into fertilizing one of them."

"Don't I know it? It's a way of life, dum-dum. It's the way of life. Like the bugs and the bees one of my primary missions in life on this earth is to pollinate."

By and by Peru reached the brain of his host.

"You won't tell anyone about my wife, will you?" said the guard.

"They don't care. Most of them have wives or girlfriends."

"Not Candress, the leader. I've seen him with women but he really hates them."

"Candress hates everybody," said Peru. "He's the only intelligent person among you."

Something in the prisoner's voice made the guard turn around. Short and stocky, breechclouted and armed with a sword, he stood staring into the black cave. His mouth quivered while his fingers were sticky upon his weapon. "Who was that? Who said that? Who's in there?"

"Your destiny." Peru stepped into the light. He resembled his dead host but was more handsome. His skin had a faint yellow tinge to it.

"Lampla! What happened to you?"

"What do you mean?"

With a gasp the guard came closer. "You look different. You've changed."

"For the better, I trust."

"Not necessarily. In fact I'm not sure I like your eyes. They're more red than green and there's yellow all around them. They remind me of something sickening."

"Believe me, I'm a definite improvement over your friend." Peru smiled with an attractive show of whitish-blue teeth. "Here, give me your hand." The guard didn't move, so the disease reached out and took hold of the appendage. His demeanor was genial, and though the guard wasn't beguiled out of his senses, he was too confused to be defensive. Taking a small piece of slate from his fiber belt, Peru made a slit in the startled man's flesh and then laid his lips to it.

Somewhere deep inside Lampla's body Disease's soul resided, minuscule in both dimension and benevolent potential.

Though he pressed the dreaded microbes into healthy flesh he by no means imparted that which was himself in the spittle. That small node remained in the host body.

The guard cried out and pulled his hand free. A yellow bubble formed on the cut, swelled, bled, began to smell bad. Even as he stared at it the sore grew and became more malevolent in appearance. He howled in pain, disgust and fear. The pestilence crept up his arm before his very eyes, splitting the skin as it went, putrefying the flesh and bones, making the blood thicker and more yellow.

He fell to the ground, wildly thrashed about for a short while before reaching for his sword and attempting to sever his arm at the elbow. He had the will but not the strength. Even as he raised the weapon to try once again the infection crawled across the wound and attacked healthy tissue.

By the time Peru decided he had witnessed sufficient of the results of his labor and walked away toward the camp, the man was nearly consumed. There were twitchings, lunges, bubblings and a myriad of stilled protests but gradually all activity ceased. With time the loathsome lump lying in front of the cave would dry out and become dust.

There were fifty woman-haters in the tribe. All but twelve had families hidden in the jungle. They didn't like Peru and knew he wasn't really Lampla but he seemed to be male and it would never have occurred to them to try to turn him away from their midst. They might be neurotic and hypocritical but never could it be said they were inhospitable.

They lived in individual ivy caves scattered along a single limb of a tree, comfortable enough homes except that they were lonely and messy. It was easy to find food and the morning dew always laid enough moisture on the leaves so that they dripped most of the day. The limb was well protected from the sun by the great bridge of strands high in the air above the tree so there was little evaporation or dehydration.

Candress especially didn't care for Lampla, primarily because the newcomer was arrogant and full of confidence. There wasn't much he could do about his dislike because after Peru thumped him on the shoulder by way of a greeting he began having severe pain in that part of him. Eventually he retreated

to his cave to rest and recuperate from a decidedly hot and
hurting case of bursitis. Or something.

Disease discovered everything there was to know about the
woman-haters and then left them to their own affairs, but not
before they were all infected with his deadly by-products. He
was learning and accumulating intelligence. It wasn't necessary
for him personally to give his enemies a dose of nastiness.
Take, for instance, Candress, who moaned and rolled about
in his cave until he got on everyone's nerves. His sore was
beginning to open and drain, just a bit, and before long someone would go in and try to lend assistance. The new man would
get infected by touching the foul matter, which had adapted
and could now swoop through pores. He would transport the
lethal cells to the others. Peru might be gone a week or even
longer before the last warrior fell amidst his own rot. It de-
pended upon how merciful the people were to one another.

They were all doomed. The criminal didn't care. Or rather
he would have cared if any survived. He intended to fulfill his
mission, the same as anyone else, and it had been dictated by
fate. Whatever one must do, one simply did. Never mind free
will. What was that but an unidentifiable pain?

Chapter 5

Whing had to go to work and cleanse the steeple of vermin. There was a never-ending horde of small and yet smaller things sneaking onto the edifice at one spot or another so that he continually had to be on the job. It was annoying to catch movement from the corner of his eye, to hear furtive scurrying, to sense the presence of pests. They never did any good but only bothered him and polluted his home. As a man, he knew his steeple was the only one on Earth still fit to handle an incoming spaceship. All the others had fallen prey to time and scavengers.

This trip he had to go nearly halfway to the ground to really scour the tower. Wherever he went life forms were routed from their places, squealing, grunting, protesting, but none of them tried resisting. Whing weighed an enormous amount that had been spawned far above the planet where there was no atmosphere.

He had a feral streak in him that he indulged whenever he cornered a hardhead. He might batter or even torture a bit before booting the trespasser out into free air. There was plenty of that and any pretenders to his throne were welcome to enough of it to force them to try their wings.

"You're too testy," Odeeda said to him during a break in his labors. "What makes you think you're good companionship?"

Whing eyed her with what he intended to be a withering expression. It would never do for her to read any admiration for her in his looks or actions because she was already bursting with self-importance. They communicated by opening and closing little flaps growing on their sides. By noisily creating puffs of air and timing the power and length of the puffing, they could allow their thoughts to be known. "I notice you're very sedentary today," he said with irascible little tootings of air. "One might think you'd laid an egg and were keeping it warm." Glowering, he stooped over in an attempt to see beneath her fat bottom. "You haven't done that, have you? Laid another egg, I mean? You know I've forbidden it."

"I remember, I haven't forgotten and I didn't do it," she said, neglecting to move over so that he could see the center of the nest. Her normal place was on a heavy cluster of strands attached to the steeple approximately a third of the way down. He didn't like her on the higher strands because she did poorly up there, failed to breathe properly and complained endlessly about the weather. In fact nobody was allowed up there. It made him feel hemmed in to have too much company, and it made him feel challenged.

"I'm going lower to clean house," he said. "See that you bear me a live child when I return. As men we only do it that way."

"I'll do my best."

The lower he went down the metal stalk the more things took to their webs, strings, vines or simply feet to get away from him. He was like a dustmop probing in the most obscure corners, disturbing and terrifying, evicting without mercy.

"And don't come back!" he tooted at them, hanging out over the clouds to watch their progress, knowing that a percentage of them would return as soon as he was gone. There was something about living high above everyone else that appealed to certain individuals, so there would always be plenty of them to harass and annoy him. It had to do with ego and the misuse of power. No matter how far the tales of his superiority carried, there were perennial younglings with more bravado than brains.

Not having an altruistic bone in his body and not caring that he hadn't, Whing did a good job of scattering nuisances living in a third or so of his highrise, after which he went back toward the top spires. By the time he arrived at his nest several weeks had gone by.

Odeeda didn't have time to hatch her egg or hide it in the strands. As she went over the side of the bridge, propelled by her mate's foot, she tucked the gem beneath a horny flap and then concentrated on locating a solid bridge somewhere in the depths below. She hadn't much maneuvering ability but the lack wasn't so drastic since there was a plenitude of spans.

She came to a bouncing rest near a bloody-headed savage of beautiful green and yellow colors, long body and intelligent emerald eyes. Instead of trying to beat her up or throw her out this male scrutinized her, examined her all over and then proceeded to wash her face with a rough tongue. He tried to tell her he was an ornad while she attempted to impart the information that she was a steeple sentry but their tootings of air were foreign to each other.

No matter, the universal language of affection and mutual approbation was sufficient and they both settled down for a nap. There was no holding back on either side as far as secrets were concerned, with a single exception. Odeeda kept her egg hidden and never let the ornad know of its existence.

Meanwhile Whing grew weary of waiting for her to return and went looking for her. It never occurred to him that she might have fallen to her death and now lay broken and crushed somewhere on the land. No, she was safely planted somewhere like a huge blue bruise, ensconced in comfort on someone's pad. It had happened before, many times. In fact, kicking her out of the nest and waiting for her to climb back up was an activity he engaged in with regularity. She hadn't the decency to come home after he evicted her but always lagged until he went after her.

This time he discovered her quite low to the ground, no more than a few thousand feet up on a strand with an ornad, and a crippled one at that. This beast looked as if he had stuck the side of his head in a meat grinder and there was Odeeda washing his wounds with her tongue.

Dark thoughts crossed Whing's mind. What had she done with the blasted egg? And while he was on the subject, whose egg was it? How could it be his when his young man was supposed to be born alive and kicking?

Such questions confused him. Though he always punished Odeeda for laying eggs he usually saw what hatched from them, and the younglings bore a disconcerting resemblance to him. Were they a mixture of ornad or some other foreigner, wouldn't they look out of the ordinary and not exactly like Odeeda's husband?

Scratching his head in anger, he hung to the side of the steeple and watched his wife and the ornad. As usual she was making a fool of herself dancing and showing off by rolling like a ball. If he fetched her now she would insult and taunt him all the way back up to the nest. Not to mention that she might not want to come. He wasn't in the mood for a quarrel. Besides, beating up on his wife would be unmanly of him. Added to that, she was too big for him to beat up.

Into hospitable reaches he climbed slowly and morosely, thinking that Odeeda complicated his life to an extent that was nearly intolerable. If it hadn't been that he missed her when she was gone he would have put her out of his mind and his life.

Clinging to a girder, he hung out as far as possible and bellowed at the top of his lungs. From a far distance came an answering cry, deep and belligerent. Probably a scrate. Conceivably another sentry, though they never grew as large as Whing. Imagine one of his scrawny cousins inviting him to war.

With a full-throated roar he swung back and forth on the girder and even thumped his chest with a fist. Again a faint answer wafted across the miles, uninhibited by thick atmosphere. Up here it was thin and clean. Whing hadn't the sense to realize that the acceptor of his challenge was on a nearby bridge. Not that it mattered. There were no wars fought down here on the strands by the giants of the sky.

Infuriated because his insult had engendered a response, he made haste toward the summit of his turf. Meanwhile other creatures heard the scrate on the bridge and took up the cry, passed it along to the next steeple that housed several denizens.

Not all the creatures within earshot of the call to arms were space warriors and not everyone was free that day, so the number of those who headed for the steeple top was about twenty. The majority were distracted before reaching their destination while others decided they weren't in the mood for a fight. Some remembered they were hungry, a few recalled their aching heads or hides, others just plain forgot what they were about. Of those who had intended to go to war only four lifted off the steeple tip.

Fat, heavy, cumbersome, vividly colored, winged or not, multi-legged, multi-eyed, skin like steel leather or leathery steel, shelled or pronged, they were all different and, like Whing, rushed to the arena with thundering hearts and cascading blood.

Whing didn't bother going inside the steeple where artificial atmosphere would have allowed him to climb at a sedate pace nearly to the top. Instead he stayed where he was and fought against the planet's gravity, pulled and hauled with his mighty arms. He didn't care if physics demanded that he travel at twenty-five thousand miles an hour and be of a certain mass and weight to escape that tremendous pull. He was a sentry, born and bred in a kind of briarpatch in a hidey hole forty thousand miles above the sod of home. He didn't care about natural law, so he pulled and hauled his incredible body up through clouds that felt like dense cheese. Thicker and heavier grew the cheese but he grew even heavier and forced his way through.

Gradually the way grew easier, became less dense and even perforated. He worked his way into the openings and through them and then all at once he let go of the girder and leaped up several hundred yards. Like a blissful tune or a frothy feather he sailed weightlessly, sublime.

To the top he went and spread his arms to the sky. While he held onto the steeple with his feet he beat his chest and screamed his mighty war cry. There was no sound. The moon blazed at him from over his shoulder while the sun disgorged yellow brimstone miles into space. He twisted back and forth on his perch, staring, probing darkness with his eyes, watching for the first antagonist to make an appearance. The little holes in his ears were closed now by a strong membrane. Likewise his large eyes were protected by a heavy, transparent sheath that permitted him full vision and even a special kind of sight. It would be a long while before he had to go back down where the air blew.

Back and forth on the shiny metal edge he swayed, rocked to and fro by every motion he made. Then he saw it, saw her, the huge scrate rising in the sunlight like a mutated phoenix, black and fearsome in silhouette against the burning moon. Her wings useless and even unnecessary now, the scrate hastened to the place of war by blowing puffs of air from tubes in her sides. She was the fastest thing aloft these days but her weapons weren't the best and so she wasn't the most formidable of contestants. Still her beak was capable of denting the hardest of armor and occasionally her claws could scratch an eye or a vulnerable section of neck or underbelly.

Tooting, sailing through vacuum like the prow of a ship, Scrate headed toward the steeple and the blowgart named Whing. Blue boob. Senseless sentry. Scrate was full of zest and confidence. It had been too long since anyone sounded the challenge. She hadn't the foresight to sound it herself and thereby put an end to the sabbatical of peace. Now it was fight time. The bout would soon begin, just as soon as she really got into perfect position, tooted a little harder to build up her speed, and then to the fore!

Behind her came Quell, slower, more ominous in appearance. He was a huge round creature with two curved antennae sticking from the top of his head. His rear end was small and knobby. He had been outflown, outmaneuvered and battered by Scrate during their last fight and so even though he traveled toward the steeple where Whing waited he in truth had it in mind to inflict damage upon the winged warrior. One thing he couldn't stand was a female who never shut her mouth and Scrate filled that bill better than anyone he knew.

From out of a pocket of black mist came the huge and lumbering Talion. She had just laid an egg in a secret place on the old steeple and worried that she might be destroyed in the flight and not make it back to witness the birth of her youngling. Still, she never hesitated to go out and meet the enemy. Red and gray in color, she supported a shell that was nearly impervious to attack. Her head poked out at an eager angle while all around her protective covering feet with nails like rapiers made swimming motions. The motions were all show. Talion could have swam in vacuum until doomsday without generating any propulsion. Her maneuvering power came from between her toes where small holes allowed gas to escape. The longer she went without air the more gas built up inside her internal organs. By the time the space battles drew to an end she was usually flying rings around her opponents but because of her lack of confidence she was seldom a winner. Rarely was she ever damaged either so there was no good reason why she worried about her egg. It would have taken more than the other three giants to crack her shell.

The victory honor was usually reserved for Whing who either hadn't the brains to know when he was outmatched or had more than his share of ego. Now he gave a silent whoop and pushed off from the steeple in a straight line toward Scrate. He slowed and drifted a bit because the big bird was more interested in the beast behind her and had sailed off course.

Silhouetted against the melting sun, the giants whirled and circled like buzzards over an invisible carcass, dipping, swaying, darting in to attack and then quickly retreating. Whing had hold of tail feathers in one hand while he attempted to bite one of Quell's antennae. The horn was like malleable metal and slid away from him, leaving not so much as a bit of skin in his teeth.

Quell turned and tried to ram Talion, who grappled with Whing and attempted to claw furrows in the sentry's blue back. Mouths opened to grunt and groan, flaps fluttered to emit gas, eyes bulged behind protective lids and breathing was suspended until the need for air superseded the glory of combat. They were a silent motion picture and none would have said the fun of what they were doing outweighed all else, but it was true. Hatred was a pretense, as were savagery and callousness.

Quell lost a nail somewhere, just a small one in comparison with the great cry he gave. It was a noiseless complaint and Scrate knew she had scored only by the way the great humped creature's mouth yawned wide. Meanwhile her rear feathers were being gnawed by Whing who never gave quarter, not even when the three ganged up on him. They always grew annoyed by his persistent and skillful attacks. Plainly he had few esthetic appreciations and didn't enjoy it when the others momentarily left the battle to do some calisthenics in view of the starlight.

One of Talion's eyes was bruised by a ramming antenna. Maddened more by smarting pride than pain, she turned on Quell and clasped the beast in her many arms. Meantime a drill-like weapon on her belly worked at piercing the fuzzy brown flesh. Bucking and kicking, Quell managed to free himself and then rammed her again. Talion went bulleting away into a blackness of swirling dust and hurtling debris.

She didn't come back. The others saw her circle far out of fighting range and then she headed back toward her steeple. Perhaps she was running out of gas or it could be that thoughts of her egg encouraged her to call it quits. It never entered the heads of the others that she might be injured, and in fact she was not. Nature had seen to it that nothing short of global disaster could harm the giants. In fact Talion had drifted so far from the arena that she forgot about the battle. Time was meaningless to her because there was always enough of it to do whatever she wanted. Now she hurried home to wait for another day and another challenge.

Scrate hadn't had enough and hurried to battle Quell who in turn was trying to outmaneuver Whing. The three met in a head-on collision that sent them in different directions. Quickly they hurried to a meeting place again, crossed paths and grappled. Quell was in the middle and had a horn yanked by Scrate's beak. As always he felt the pressure deep down inside his head and gave a roar of protest. His horns grew into his brain and he had no intention of being rendered simple-minded by an overgrown bird.

There she was, laughing at him, because she had seen his mouth open to sound a bellow. Ignoring Whing who chewed at his knobby tail, he darted forward and took hold of a mouthful of feathers. Immediately Scrate gave a soundless howl and used her deadly feet to scrape away her attacker. It did no good. Quell was an insensitive sort and didn't really mind the clawing. His hide had withstood and would withstand more than that before he was done.

He didn't let loose when Scrate gave the surrender signal. Gleeful and unrelenting, he hung on even after she abandoned the arena and headed home. Through the sky they went, the scrate tooting and scratching and the quell hanging on, belly-up and tenacious.

Whing floated on his back and watched them leave. There was more camaraderie among the other denizens because they lived together on the ruined steeple a thousand miles west of his own. He could have gone after the two and even visited their skyscraper but eventually there would have been a brawl and he would come home bruised and weary. Better that he stayed aloof. That way he could maintain his reputation and not get into too many fights. Once in a while was fine but more than that was for younglings.

Long after his acquaintances had disappeared he stared at the area in space where he had last seen them. Slowly he began to move. In a long and lazy arc he sailed in front of the moon's backdrop. Around and around in space he went, looping, dipping, swimming, skipping, his body keeping pace with inaudible music in his brain. He was an adventurer who saw strange things done, who went forth to pit his might against the inscrutable. There were thoughts of grace and beauty and lilting tunes, perhaps a ballroom and a lady fair whose bodily proportions never became clear in his mind. At leisure he danced by the light of the moon, not caring that the sun had already dawned on Earth.

Chapter 6

"You have no right to keep the wig!" said Pip. He and Kadooka stood on a leaf twenty feet in diameter and a foot think. All around them the forest green glittered in the sunlight. His head was sore and his legs were shaky but he stood firmly enough on the limb and tried to stand up to Kadooka. It wasn't easy to do when he wanted to fall down and sleep. He had to get away, though, before LaLa got her hooks into him too securely. For a week she had nursed him and it was nearly enough to make him forget his profession and his desire to be footloose.

"I never said I was keeping it, did I?" Kadooka tossed the scalp to the younger man and grinned. "Though you aren't keeping it either if you don't finish the job. I don't pay for unfinished business."

"I did more to that monster than anyone else you've ever seen or heard tell of!"

"True. I thought sure he was a goner when you cut that string he was on, which is why I'm letting you hold onto the wig until you make your second try." As Pip started to move away the big man added, "Get any thoughts out of your head about sneaking away permanently with my property. I can track you anywhere and if I have to come and get you I'll break a couple of your bones."

"I just need a little time to myself."

"That suits me fine. I don't want you hanging around here making eyes at LaLa."

45

"I never made eyes at her!"

"I suppose you think it was the other way around? Don't kid yourself.. She has better taste than you and so do I. When she gets married it'll be to a good catch. Now beat it and get back here in a week or two to take care of that bridge beast, otherwise I'll stomp you into a swamp."

So much for threats and regrets. Pip intended to get lost in the wilderness and never see Kadooka or his sister again. He wasn't confident or happy about it, though. Why couldn't he shake the feeling that the big man was capable of backing up every word he said?

Walking to the end of a limb, he jumped out onto a plateau of green moss. He knew exactly how far away the ground was but had no desire to go down there. It was infested with gas-belching creatures that marauded night and day and who fortunately weren't good climbers. Everything with that talent had already visited the big trees and lower bridges. Those that didn't like what they found returned to the surface, while others hid in various places and lay in wait for something edible to happen along.

Pip passed a siren of awesome size skulking in an alcove of ivy. Its song wafted out to him on the damp morning air and he was almost compelled to go closer. It was the same every time. Whenever he heard the voice of the deadly plant his initial reaction was to submit, but then his more intelligent brain warned him away.

Here and there on the plateau were little puddles that made grumbling and growling sounds, or there were crawling leaves that suddenly took flight on wings or gossamer webs. At times he passed entire sections of moss that heaved and throbbed with life. The air was filled with birds, some large enough to consider trying to snap him up. He swung his sword to drive them off. To his right was what looked like a mountain of green foliage where small or gross things of many colors clambered and fought. It wasn't a mountain at all but a drooping section of a bridge. On his left a fogbank prowled across the moss and sneaked up into the top branches of a huge tree.

Like a sloppy web the strings and strands crossed from bridge point to bridge point, down to the trees, back up to another strand, over to a dangling patch of strings and back up to the main span. For a thousand miles it stretched like gruesome paint flung from an artist's brush, dripping in some places, desert-dry in others, eternal like the sun's heat that was captured beneath.

It was a good place to live. It was the only place to live. Farther east was the ocean and another bridge that ran into the fog like a swaying drunk, huge and shaggy. What had built that particular span Pip didn't know and never tried to find out. Meeting the creator out on foggy strands high above thrashing water was an idea that couldn't appeal to him.

Now he walked with caution and tried to make his two eyes do the work of eight. It wasn't a strain to travel in territory that was familiar to him. It was very like home turf. Everywhere he had been was like home. Walking in it was simply a matter of keeping all senses alert.

Once he stopped to pick a fruit and threw it at the creature that had followed him from Kadooka's place. It was the freak snape, the one with the white eye and scarred head. The fruit came nowhere near it but it got the message and faded back into obscurity. It didn't abandon the train but remained far enough in the background that the man didn't grow too annoyed.

Pip took the wig from his belt and put it on. Immediately invisible rays dived into his brain to furnish him with happiness. For a while he was compelled to hide in a clean cavity in the moss to indulge himself in pleasure, but finally he returned the wig to his belt and continued his journey. Kadooka would track him a long way before giving up, so he must travel rapidly for at least several days. It was true that the big man didn't seem to be behind him on the trail. No matter, Kadooka would do what he had threatened, or at least part of it. He wouldn't let Pip get away without a struggle. It was up to the younger man to see that he was the winner in this contest of wills and tracking finesse.

Sunset found him in the glades where the footing was treacherous and where croaking things the size of stumps kept him alert. They ate whatever moved and since he couldn't outrun them, especially in the dark, he decided to burrow inside a mound of leaves and there he slept until dawn. Then he crept between the great sleeping animals and was out of their territory before daylight opened their eyes.

Toward noon he met a hunter trying to spear a cremont with an arrow-thin javelin made of shale. The weapon hadn't been made well, was tip-heavy and landed a foot in front of the bushy-tailed game. It leaped three feet into the air, twisted toward a strand of ivy and scampered into the brush before the hunter could even think about retrieving his weapon. Her weapon?

The stranger was bedecked from chin to ankle in blooming plant skin so that Pip couldn't tell whether he was male or female. Since he liked knowing which he was talking to, he asked, after the amenities were taken care of and he felt he could be a bit more personal.

"Am I what?" said the stranger. The voice was low and pleasant, but was it too high for a man's or too low for a woman's?

Pip thought it was weird. Men generally could be distinguished from females, at least before middle age when features tended to fade, blend and meld and when nobody really cared anyhow. But this stranger remained an unknown.

"We're descoes," said the hunter. "Descoes like their privacy. Please don't get intimate." He could have been a she but Pip never did find out since this particular member of the ill-fated tribe didn't live long enough to reveal anything so personal as her or his gender. In fact it probably wouldn't have mattered if he-she had survived. Pip still wouldn't have learned the secret.

They were all like that, the entire tribe of people. From birth children were raised in a commune by individuals other than their mothers, and always their bodies remained covered. No one knew who gave birth, no one knew who their children were, and likewise no one could tell the girls from the boys after they were old enough to know to keep their clothes on.

"We had a sex war a long time ago and this is the way we solved it," said one of the tribe members to Pip after he agreed to handle some murders for them. In exchange they gave him a basketful of beautifully carved jewelry made of jade, turquoise and gold.

"How do you know whom to marry? I mean, when you want to love someone? I mean—"

"I know what you mean. Believe me, it works out, though it takes a bit of time. Of course, only the couple is aware, but naturally it's a secret between them."

In Pip's opinion the descoes were fools not simply to have gone on living and let nature run its course. War? In the beginning it had to have been waged by a skitzy fringe. Unfortunately when the saner majority heard the battle squeals, they mistook them for full blown bellows and chose sides.

The descoes did have a problem, or rather another unrelated problem. Someone or something was decimating their ranks and had been doing so for several months, taking one or two citizens at a time, often at night, devouring parts of the corpses and leaving the remainder where it would shock the survivors. A group of hunters had either killed or driven off all the predators in the surrounding area but that didn't stop the murders.

Pip was assigned an ivy tent but he preferred to stay in the open by the campfire. The extra heat wasn't necessary but the descoes were lovers of light and built a glowing mound of twigs and logs every sundown.

Pip had been there two full days when the ganute attacked him. He wasn't even investigating at the time but was picking berries from a bush growing in a wide corridor of vines. The creature hit him from the rear and knocked him on his face. He felt something gnawing at his neck and fought back in terror for several minutes before realizing that while he was being mauled he wasn't being hurt. Managing to roll onto his back he looked up into the most frightening face he had ever seen, black and woolly with three white eyes and a gaping blue mouth. There were no teeth in the hungry orifice that made munching motions along his ribs. Neither were there any nails on the forepaws or feet. The animal was as impotent as a fangless serpent.

The ganute had been defanged and declawed as a cub after the descoes killed his mother in the sponge cave beyond the ivy corridor. Now the half-grown creature acted out his feelings of agression by attacking everyone he saw, who at that moment happened to be Pip.

With the animal practically on his back, he staggered to the camp where the descoes hauled it off him and booted its rear until it rambled away. With much growling and snarling it retreated into the forest.

One of the natives brought Pip a bowl of berries. "That beast won't go away," he-she said. "No matter how much we persecute it, it hangs around."

"Can you blame him?" said Pip. "You've made a flower out of him. How long could he survive out there in the world?"

"You must understand that I had nothing to do with maiming it." The descoe was the same one Pip had met in the swamp. His or her name was Taroo.

"Did you object while it was being done?"

"What do you mean?"

"Somebody mutilated him. Did you try to stop them?"

"They didn't do it just for entertainment. The creature who reproduced him-her had to be killed because looking at her-him was offensive. Besides it was dangerous and threatened our safety. It made no attempt to hide the fact that it had given birth. Ugh!"

Pip put on the wig because the conversation was doing nothing positive for him. Relaxing, he said, "But as an animal such an act would never occur to her."

"There's always the example. Once we set it we expect the populace to follow it." When Pip stirred uncomfortably, Taroo casually added, "That doesn't include you. We know there are other tribes with different cultural philosophies. If you weren't an insurance salesman but just a common person who wanted to stay and live with us you'd have to hide your body in a plant skin."

"But everyone would know I'm a man."

"We'd pretend we didn't know and eventually we would forget."

"Just like that?"

Taroo nodded. "Life is simple."

"By the way, there's something else I noticed about the ganute. Somebody castrated him."

"We put clothes on it to hide its identity but it kept taking them off. What else was there to do? It wasn't a hasty decision. We had a meeting first."

Pip slept on this tidbit of information and decided that, jewelry or no jewelry and wig or no wig, he would leave the descoes before they decided to make an example of him.

In the morning he was by the fire, eating roasted cremont when the ganute jumped on his back and began gumming his head. Pounding the creature with a club, he made it leave off and then he fed it meat, which it ate bones and all.

He half-cooked another cremont and the creature greedily consumed it. Then, not at all grateful, it attacked him again and nearly knocked him into the fire. The noise attracted the attention of several descoes who came out and threw rocks and javelins at the furry beast until he retreated to the sponge cave. There he sprawled in the opening, growling and snarling with ferocity, pretending that he was a fully capable ganute. At least he was full of food.

"Maybe he really is killing your people," Pip said to Taroo at the meeting. The descoes held one every day before noon.

Taroo shook his-her head. "We thought of that and we considered doing away with the beast but the consensus of opinion was against the idea. There are those of us who believe we've done enough to it. Not that we wouldn't kill it if it was the murderer, but it isn't. It eats small animals like cremonts but it can't chew up a human body. We've given it parts of corpses. It tries to eat them but it simply can't."

That took care of that. Thinking of jewelry and a murderer who committed frightful atrocities upon its victims, Pip considered taking off while he was still in one piece. With his pay.

Those days too many people seemed to be able to read minds. The leader of the people cornered Pip and said to him, "Don't get any ideas about skipping out, with or without the jewelry. It won't matter to us which. You accepted our hospitality which we don't offer liberally. Now you must fulfill your obligation to us by finding the killer who's depleting our ranks."

"What happens if I fail for any reason? I am fallible, you know."

"Better not be this time. Think of the ganute."

Was that a threat? Pip wondered. Certainly it had to be. Either he found the murderer among the descoes or there would be two defanged characters sponging off them.

The thing of it was that he had no real bravado and this was because he had been bred among carnivores bigger and stronger than he. Only in his head did he outmatch the life forms around him, but that was scarcely ever enough. It had always seemed sufficient to growl back at an enemy and perhaps chuck a spear in its direction while he was in retreat.

"How long has it been since the last victim was found?" he asked Taroo.

"The night before you came. Six nights ago. Actually it might not have been that long since the killer struck. A hunter who was supposed to come home three days ago hasn't. Also a water carrier disappeared yesterday. We've been looking for them but we haven't found a trace."

"Does the killer usually leave any, uh, of the victim?"

"Yes, it's almost as if he-she is doing it on purpose. Always there's a head or a foot, or something."

"So if the hunter and the water carrier are dead we're bound to find a remain?"

"Yes."

The next day an arm was found sticking in a mound of mud behind the farthest ivy tent. Someone identified it as the hunter's. That evening the head of the water carrier was discovered in the dampened campfire.

"This is truly arrogance, to say the least," said Pip to Taroo. "The killer is unafraid. He's coming right out into the open."

"Unfortunately he-she knows our habits. She-he is fully aware that we take a nap an hour before dinner."

"The thing to do is post a guard."

"We can't do that."

"Why not?" said Pip.

"You must be aware that we have total equality among us."

"That means if you're all taking naps, you're all doing it."

"Yes."

"How about equality with an occasional sacrifice? If you post a guard you probably won't find any more heads or arms in your campfire."

"We hired you so we wouldn't need to make sacrifices."

The ganute wasn't proficient at climbing trees but he climbed one anyhow during the evening repast and threw fruit at the diners. A squad of them was sent to knock him off his perch, after which he was stoned until he ran away to his cave. As punishment he would get no dinner. He must have been accustomed to it. The descoes were skilled at depriving him of one thing or another.

"Really he-she seems not to care at all about food," said Taroo to Pip. "She-he is always doing things like that. I'm surprised he-she stays so fat."

"I've seen him run. He's very fast. He can catch a cremont if he gets it out in the open."

"It's much too heavy to be truly speedy. If it really got itself into shape it might go off into the wilderness and be self-sufficient. That would take a big strain off us. We don't enjoy having it around."

"It isn't possible," said Pip.

"What makes you think you know so much?"

Staring at the smooth and genderless face, Pip wondered and gave an inward shrug. What did he care if this person was a boy or a girl? Perhaps they were right after all. It didn't matter unless one was romantically inclined, which he wasn't. So far he had been in the camp a little less than two weeks and in all that time he had ice water in his veins. He didn't even like any of them, not even this one, who spoke of life as if it were something to be twisted or ignored.

"I've been out in the world most of my life," he said. "Ever since my parents were killed when a bridge string collapsed. I know there's no way the ganute can survive out there. What you people did to him was unconscionable. Death would have been more merciful."

Taroo never batted an eye. "You're a stranger and we make allowances for you, but don't be too outspoken or noisy in your criticism. There are those among us with little tolerance for heresy. The ganute was treated as it was because we were attempting to civilize it. The failure didn't lie with us, but we learned never to try it again with an inferior species. The next time we'll simply kill any intruder."

That marked the end of real conversation between the descoes and their insurance salesman. Life must have been tedious for them, or so Pip thought, and all because some skitzy females in the past were ashamed of the fact that they had babies, or some skitzy males hated the idea of being labeled as fathers. Probably both had been true. As was often the case with human beings, the ones who yelled the loudest had the most influence; when the day came that everybody felt safe enough to raise their heads and take a look around, they discovered just how much their world had changed.

Not that Pip was concerned with history. For the first time in weeks he thought of LaLa and how comfortable it had been to be in her presence and have her tend his wound. There was a bluish-white scar on his right temple to remind him of his meeting with the ornad. Somehow the memory didn't disturb him so much now that he had met the descoes and their kicking boy, the ganute.

Chapter 7

Since everyone kept an eye on him so that he couldn't sneak away, Pip pretended to investigate by poking about in the sponge cave. For all he knew he would find a secret exit somewhere in it. It was an awesome and huge enclosure that had been washed up by the ocean millennia earlier. Somehow the living thing inside it managed to get this far from the water before expiring, and there sat its shell at the end of the corridor of ivy, oblong with a gaping mouth like an enormous whale head.

Over the years stalactites and stalagmites formed humps and lumps that captured gloom or shine and deposited them partway toward the back partition or along the sides. The walls were rough like sandpaper and dotted with thorny knobs.

From mouth to rear of the cave was a span of approximately three hundred yards. The width was nearly as much. Here and there the floor had either been dug away or had rotted so that occasional pits and chuckholes made footing treacherous. Along the back was total darkness and it was the place Pip liked to be least of all. It didn't smell bad there in the blackness nor were there any disturbing sounds. It simply seemed to be inhabited by all the forbidden fragments of his imagination.

The descoes seldom went into the cave. For one thing the ganute lived there, and for another their imaginations were even more fertile than that of their insurance man. All their phobias and secret torments seemed to swim nearer to the surface of their psyches with every step they took into the fearful depths of the sea cadaver. Perhaps faint echoes of pounding surf reverberated among the dead cells or it might have been that the shell merely provided a backboard for guilty consciences. At any rate they confessed their terrors to one another and avoided the place.

The first time Pip entered he came to an abrupt halt as the ganute rose up among the rock dunes to snarl at him. For a change it didn't bellow and charge to the attack but only stared at him until he went away.

Later he saw it down by a stream running along a culvert in a huge tree limb. As soon as it spied him it reared up on its hind legs and sounded a battle cry. Maybe the only neutral territory it recognized was the cave or maybe it had been hoping he would go deeper inside its home where it could corner him. Now he didn't wait but beat a hasty retreat back to the camp.

The descoes didn't needle him or display signs of impatience that the days were passing and the corpses were piling up. Plainly they intended to grant him sufficient time in which either to satisfy them or hang himself.

Sometimes the killings took place in the daytime and once the ganute was in a tree over Pip's head when a blood-curdling cry came from the direction of the stream. All the descoes ran into their caves and left Pip to face the crisis alone. He would have gone into his own home but the ganute dropped from the tree and barred his path. The creature seemed to know how afraid he was. Curiosity finally got the better of him and he went down to the stream, but first he armed himself with a stone javelin of his own making.

A woman lay draped over a tree limb with her headless self dripping into the void below a hole in the moss plateau. Her plant skins had been ripped from her body. Since the descoes didn't seem to consider underground interment or cremation as a necessary treatment of the spirit's house, he tipped the body off the limb and directed it down into the hole. He was listening for a sound he knew he would never hear—that of her landing on the surface far below— when a noise behind him made him straighten and whirl. There was the ganute crouching on an ivy mound watching him. It didn't look hostile or even unfriendly and in fact he thought the expression on its face might have been that of interest or curiosity. He couldn't be sure, besides which he didn't really care. What captured and held his attention was the creature's bloody muzzle.

The descoes didn't like the theories he presented upon his return to the camp. As far as they were concerned he had ganute on the brain and was getting on their nerves with his dumb ideas. Of course the murderer wasn't one of them and of course it had to be a marauding animal. No, they didn't mind that he had disposed of the corpse by dumping it through the moss but they minded horridly when he mentioned her gender. They had known the deceased for fifty or more years but only at a superficial level and that was the way they would have wished the relationship to end.

Somewhere in their midst a citizen found cause to burst into tears when he-she heard the news but her-his emotional display was totally ignored. One might have thought it didn't even happen.

Into the sponge cave Pip tramped with his javelin in hand. He intended to corner the ganute, scare or bully it into submission so that he could get a vine around its neck, and then he planned to tether it until the descoes realized no more murders were being committed. Somehow this beast was the guilty party.

He tried laying a rope on a wolverine, not that he had ever been face to face with such a species, but the nature of the two beasts was similar. The ganute had been snuffling and rooting in a dark hole through which a cremont had run and when Pip tapped it on the rear end with his javelin it came up and about like an avenger.

Strangely it stopped snarling as soon as it saw him, and it made an attempt to assume a benign facade, but not before he got a good look at its fangs and unsheathed claws. The latter were like curved daggers while the former could have snapped off his head with a single closing.

Weakened nearly to the point of swooning, certain that he was being followed and was going to be ripped to shreds, he staggered back along the ivy corridor and across the field to the camp with his tale. He needn't have wasted his breath. The descoes didn't believe him and made open fun of him.

"You haven't a great deal of character," Taroo said to him.

"Is that so? At least I didn't run when the woman screamed."

"Watch your language. You've had sufficient warning about that. And why shouldn't we protect ourselves? We've paid you to fight our battles for us."

"Do you admit that the ganutes are your mortal enemies?"

Taroo remained unruffled, as did his-her companions. "Certainly neither I nor anyone will admit to such nonsense," she-he said. "You think to coax us into doing away with our wretched creature so you can leave with your treasure. You shouldn't take us for such complete fools."

Holding his hand, Pip knelt by the fire and groaned. "She gave birth to two cubs, don't you understand? Not one. The mother ganute—"

"How disgusting. Stop such talk at once. Really, this time you've gone too far."

They dragged him into the sponge cave and tied him to a rocky stalk. All the while he tried to make them see the error of their ways.

"There you are," said Taroo. "Sorry about this but you've got to learn how to speak in our presence. Until you know how to be less offensive you'll stay here."

"Wait, wait!" he said. "Listen to me. You hired me, didn't you? Well, I did the job, and I'm telling you there are two ganutes and the healthy one is getting bigger every day. Twins, do you hear?"

They went away and left him and by and by monster number two came out of the deep tunnel she had bored in the back wall. Pip took one look at her in the dimness and fainted. When he came to she was gone. Sagging against the post, he perspired and prayed and listened for some sign that the future might be hastening his way.

Toward evening the monster returned with a victim in tow. Having silenced the man by dethroating him, the potent ganute dragged the wriggling thing to a spot in the cave where Pip could have a clear view. Then she ripped away the clothing and ate it.

Praying out loud, gagging, weeping, Pip strained against his bonds. The ganute seemed to have no grudge against him.

She obviously recognized him and now she was talking to him about the sweetness of revenge. She had seen her mother murdered. The beloved one hadn't had time to hide her male child, only the female. For months the whole pup remained in hiding and witnessed the degradation of her brother. At night she hunted for food. Time went by and she grew. As soon as her weapons were sufficiently developed she began wiping out the tribe of descoes. Now she wanted the non-desco to understand that if he wished to survive he was to mind his own business and stay out of the battle.

By the time the scene was done Pip understood everything she had to say and was willing to sneak away at the first opportunity, without treasure or anything else the ganute dictated. He experienced more horrifying sounds when the creature padded behind him and chewed his bonds until they fell loose.

At that moment someone outside approached. In a flash the animal fled down a hole while Pip stood dry-eyed and stiff. The floor of the cave was clean. The victim was all consumed and the clothes lay behind a rock.

"Just checking to see if you're all right," said Taroo. He-she raised a gourd to Pip's mouth so he could drink. "We have a most interesting visitor," he-she continued. "Named Peru. An odd person, indeed. At first he was male and then gradually he became neuter, almost as if he wanted to please us. A changee, I think. I've heard of them but this is the first time I've had the pleasure of meeting one."

"So that's it? That's your dream? To become neuter?"

"Of course. But not just me. It has to happen to everybody."

"Naturally. A lunatic hates solitude."

Taroo wasn't offended or even vexed. "If we convert the world we won't be lunatics. We'll be the normal majority."

"Wait. Don't go. There's something I have to tell you. I can help you. It's about the ganutes. Wait! Wait!"

He-she walked away without looking back and left Pip to wonder what he should do. The people would be all over the place because of the visitor. They'd be at the stream, around the campfire, in the orchards, under the arbors, which meant he couldn't get away now. He would have to wait. And if the ganute decided he was an enemy after all?

At nightfall he crawled from the cave and almost ran head-long into the monster. Soundlessly he was pushed down into the tall grass and, stretched out beside the sinister animal, he watched those in the camp. He could see the brother ganute, the harmless one. It lay in a tree above the firesite, silent and interested in the stranger who sat on a basket and told stories.

Peru was naked and genderless. He was scarcely human. His chest was without any marks of breasts and he had no navel. When he stood up and turned around, as he often did, he revealed that his body had no anal opening. He was totally neuter which actually meant that he wasn't anybody, but the descoes were too narrowminded to admit the fact to themselves or each other. He looked exactly as each of them believed others ought to look.

Peru was more yellow than usual this night or it could have been that the full moon had chosen to light him up like a dim candle. His eyes were demonic coals, more vivid than the embers in the fire, as depthless as Hades and far less restful. A spawn of the pit, he naturally sought out that which was most complimentary to himself or that which was most like him. In this case it was the tribe of descoes.

One of the people did a frenetic dance around the flames after the storyteller kissed him on the cheek, quite a pinching little manifestation of affection that broke the skin. The others didn't realize what was happening to the man's head until it swelled up like a balloon, exploded and hurled bloody filth everywhere.

Several descoes leaped up and ran straight toward the place where Pip lay in hiding. The ganute killed two of them and the survivors ran back to the fire where three or four of their neighbors were dancing by the light in the sky. The tribe had been so meticulous about fencing up the camp exits that now there weren't enough ways of escape.

Like a gentleman dispensing favors, Peru moved among his hosts and clawed their flesh with a fingernail filed and honed to a glittering point. He needn't have been so personal but preferred it tonight. He seemed to want all of life at once and

didn't wish anyone to crawl away to die a dignified death.
Dignity was beneath him.

The potent ganute was intelligent and realized it when someone was trying to steal her thunder. Out of the forest she sprang
with all weapons formidably in the fore. Here a desco lost her
skirt and her lower half, there another had his leg ripped from
him. In confusion the latter crawled to Peru who held out a
hand that suddenly began to drip like melted wax. The yellow
peril fell into the wound and blew the leg up like an inflated
raft in a matter of seconds.

Someone fell into the fire and the stink of corruption and
putrefaction rose on the night breeze. Backed against the fences
around the camp, the people thought about fighting back.
Rocks flew through the air. Taroo threw a javelin at the upright
murderer and this time the aim was true. The stone went straight
through Peru's body and became stuck, entered where his belly
button was normally situated, went in halfway and stayed there.
It had no effect on Peru, or it caused him no discomfort. It did
appear to amuse him for he laughed and caused yellow bacteria
to flow to both protruding ends of the weapon where it dropped
on the faces and buttocks of writhing victims.

The ganute in the tree jumped onto Peru and knocked him
down. Not lingering to be infected by a friendly finger or fang,
the animal scampered away and prowled through the woods
until it located its sister. It found Pip too and immediately
jumped on him.

Pip didn't care. The drama being played at the fire was the
only thing that mattered and he lay still while the creature
gnawed his back. By and by its sister gave it a kick. Reluctantly
it gave off trying to eat the human and lay beside him to watch.

Peru hadn't taken his eyes off Taroo since that one impaled
him with the javelin. Like a make-believe spook he spread his
arms and legs and lurched toward the desco, but this time it
was for real. He was truly a spook without conscience or
remorse. His host body stumbled forward and all at once his
arms splashed yellow dung. His sides seemed to flow, his legs
emitted a golden and red shower. Still he maintained his human
shape, or almost.

"Run!" Pip shouted to Taroo, but he couldn't be heard above

the shrieks and screams that filled the air. Again and again he cried a warning but no one heard him.

Taroo stood transfixed in horror as the runny thing swept down on him-her and gathered her-his corporeal form into a terrifying embrace. The arms opened again and Taroo leaped high in the air. Like a puppet on a string he-she jerked and danced. Like a bacon rind in hot fat she-he swelled and split, turned brown and then a glittering yellow color streaked with red. His-her eyes spilled down her-his bursting cheeks. As he-she fell dead a high scream came from her-his mouth.

The dead lay everywhere and the potent ganute was enraged because most of her revenge had been assumed by the reeking stranger. Again from her hiding place she sprang, rushed across the clearing and attacked. She was too intelligent to be murdered like the descoes. Even as Peru opened his arms to welcome another victum she sprang into space, swung her hind feet about and kicked the infection in his artificial chest. Peru stumbled backward and fell into the fire. So startled and maddened was he that he lay where he was and began to smoke and stink up the already foul air.

During the lull in the mayhem the female ganute collected her brother and together they took off for parts unknown. They would live long lives but never would they return anywhere near the land of the descoes. Used-to-be descoes.

They were all dead. Peru made certain of it. Hauling his fearsome and injured carcass from the flames, he hobbled about the area in search of something alive. Since there was no one present to care what he looked like, he was indifferent to his appearance. The back of his head was a burnt stub. His belly still supported Taroo's javelin and his legs were of various lengths. With one arm spread out like a frozen spray of liquid, he hobbled, limped and dragged over the terrain. Now and then he lifted a corpse. Once in a while he nudged one with a foot or rolled it over. He didn't seem to mind that there was no more work for him to do here. The evening was done and he had fulfilled a particle of his mission.

He was so full of confidence that his search wasn't as diligent as it ought to have been. He missed someone, a living being, an individual. He passed over a quivering human who lay beneath three bodies mutilated by the ganute. No sound of a throbbing heart reached his lazy ears, no odor of coursing blood reached his nostrils. They were already clogged with his own stink. With a smile and a shrug he walked into the forest to look for something else interesting to do.

Chapter 8

While Ferrer Burgoyne slept, DeLoona slipped into his hut and kissed him on the mouth, causing him to contract a fever that kept him incoherent for a few days. Every so often he came partially awake and stared up into her face. In his delirium he thought she was the siren plant that had wanted to eat him.

"You can't possibly be human," he said to her after his fever subsided.

"Your hair and skin are so unusual," said DeLoona. "Where do you come from? To what tribe do you belong? In a way you remind me of the mushrooms in the loam mounds but they aren't human."

Ferrer sank back onto his sponge pillow and stared about the ivy cave. "How can you live in such places? Don't you break out in a rash and itch? It would drive me mad. In fact it is driving me mad."

"Don't worry about Kadooka. His bark is worse than his bite. As long as you look weak and sick he won't run you off."

Ferrer could see that the cave was clean. That didn't make him feel any better. He kept thinking of himself as part of the stuffing in a big green pepper. Evidently the people—no, the aborigines—did nothing in their huts but sleep while the remainder of their living was done outside. As for the woman, she hadn't displayed any hostile feelings toward him but that didn't mean he could relax his guard or even look squarely at her.

"Your skin isn't human," he said, glancing at her from the

corner of his eye. "It's too shiny and smooth, like bamboo."
He shuddered and looked away. "I don't care how soft it is.
It's a plant. You're a plant. You remind me of a big dandelion
with black hair."

DeLoona offered him a slice of melon which he declined
to accept. "You'll never get your strength back if you don't
eat."

"Maybe not altogether a plant. The fact is you're all mutants.
No white in your eyes, blue teeth, skin like smooth wood. And
look how tall you are. I'm six feet but you're higher. And why
do your teeth click when you talk?" Ferrer shivered and
DeLoona promptly covered him with a blanket of soft material.
"Leave me alone," he said. "I don't want your attentions. It
disturbs me when you behave like a person. Like a woman.
It makes my stomach turn into knots." The thought of his
inward state made him suddenly have dry heaves during which
time DeLoona held his head, which only increased his fear and
nausea. "Let me be!" he groaned. "Go away and let me die
in peace. You've infected me with some ungodly disease. I
know I'm near death but why does it have to be in your presence? We can't even talk to each other."

"If we spoke the same language I'd tell you how attractive
you are." DeLoona helped him lie down again and laid cool
moss on his forehead. "Your skin is like the brown worm and
your hair is pure fluttersilk, only brighter. I even like your
eyes though they're little dark pebbles in lakes of white."

Kadooka came to stand in the cave mouth. "You spend too
much time in here."

"He's sick and needs nursing."

"If he lives or dies he doesn't need you to watch."

"I'm in love."

"You're what?"

"This is the man I'll marry."

A great scowl grew on Kadooka's face. "Why do you and
your sister have such rotten taste? This guy is a punk."

"He's lovely and brave."

"He keels over at first sight of a normal dame. I'll bet he's
from one of those weird tribes down south. The kind that hate

women. Get out of there and leave him be. Ever since you laid eyes on him you've been disobedient to me."

Ferrer hauled himself up onto his elbows. "A bear!" he croaked. "I never saw so much hair in my life! Where did you get your genes?" DeLoona tried to help him lie flat again but he shoved her away. Staring up at her, he suddenly groaned and turned away.

With a grin Kadooka said, "I'm happy and gratified to see the feelings of love in this tent aren't mutual."

"He's just upset."

"He sure is. Every time he looks at you."

A few days passed and Ferrer began to feel better. DeLoona helped him out of the hut and onto a stretch of beach where he lay basking in a sunbeam that sneaked through the bridge overhead. Actually the beach was a sandbar packed down on two limbs growing close together. The woman brought him food.

"I wouldn't be so nervous if you stopped staring at me like that," he said to her. "I suppose you want us to be friends but I simply can't. You must understand that I come from a highly civilized culture while you're just a ludicrous freak."

She knelt and studied him with a pensive expression. "How can I tell if your health is improving? Your color is so abnormal it isn't much of a gauge."

"There's nothing like you on Laredo. I'm sorry to have to tell you how inferior you are. On a scale of one to ten I'd give you a minus five. Not on your looks because that wouldn't be fair. I mean on your general, all around self. I suspect that when I'm not watching you'll attack me and probably try and offer me up to your idol as a religious sacrifice, or something."

"The whites of your eyes were a bit bloodshot yesterday. Now they're clear and shiny. Maybe I can use them as a gauge."

"If you turn out to be benign I guess maybe we'll be friends of a sort. Like Crusoe and Friday. But not for long. If I live I've an important mission to perform for mankind."

For some reason his words made him glum and he fell silent. He wouldn't eat but lay staring up at a patch of foliage. He didn't even notice when she went away and left him alone. It was too hot, like a steambath one moment and a desert the next, and he was relieved when it started to rain. DeLoona ran down the limb from her cave and tried to make him come back inside. She seemed quite agitated and he wondered if there was about to be a cloudburst or some other natural disaster.

"I don't care, I hope I drown!" he said and shoved her away. A big drop fell on his leg and she suddenly fell to her knees to stare at it. She seemed astonished when it remained on his skin in a clear, round bubble. A few drops fell on her own arm and she showed Ferrer how they immediately seeped into her and disappeared. At once his stomach turned queasy and he refused to look at her again.

She ran back up the limb to her brother's hut and helped carry Pip to the beach. LaLa was there, too. They laid him beside Ferrer.

"He needs some kind of therapy so we're trying this," said DeLoona.

Ferrer peered into Pip's face. "What's the matter with him? He looks wiped out."

Almost as if she understood the question DeLoona said, "He's in some kind of shock. He keeps talking about the end of the world and he has fits. He staggered in here day before yesterday and he's very sick."

Pip gave a loud shriek and sat up. LaLa pushed him back down and stroked his brow.

"We've got to do something to bring him to his senses," said DeLoona. "We've decided to give him a good soaking. Maybe a brainwashing will help."

The rain started in earnest and they all ran away to shelter, leaving Ferrer and Pip to face the downpour. Actually it didn't come down that hard, just enough to give Ferrer a warm bath. He looked over at his companion and then sat up in consternation. The mutant called Pip was soaking up the water like a sponge. His body was definitely getting larger.

A sponge holds only so much fluid and then it begins leaking. By the time this happened to Pip the rain had stopped and the others returned to take him back to his cave. He lay blinking and puffing on the sand, unable to help himself. Round and swollen like an elephant's leg, he weighed more than four hundred pounds.

"You'll have to help us," Kadooka said to Ferrer. When the latter didn't move he stuck his toes under a brown thigh. "Don't give me that no-understand, helpless junk. Get off your duff and help us haul this idiot into a cave where he can dry out slowly. Personally I hope it gives him triple pneumonia. Get up, now!"

Ferrer laid his hands on Pip's wrist, squeezed and then had to take time out to gag. It was fear that made him ill when the water gushed. If these people only looked like animals or if they only had leaves growing from their heads instead of hair he could have faced up to the situation.

Again he took his share of Pip's saturated carcass and assisted in dragging him to a cave. Behind them trailed a tide of water.

"You stay here and keep an eye on him," Kadooka said to him. He blocked the doorway as Ferrer tried to leave. Pointing at Pip he said, "Stay here and watch him. You might as well begin paying for the food you're eating."

In resignation the human sat beside the unconscious man. It was difficult to say if his companion was sleeping or dead. Certainly he ought to be the latter, that is if he was in any way normal, which he wasn't. One could only marvel that he hadn't broken apart in sections while he was being dragged up here from the beach.

Once in a while DeLoona passed by the hut, glanced in and smiled or waved. Ferrer laid his head on his knees and groaned. There was no doubt in his mind that he was being courted. He wept for a number of reasons: he had cause, it was in his nature to do so when distressed though he usually fought the urge, and there was nobody important here to see him do it.

"Help!" said Pip in a soggy voice. Water dribbled from his mouth.

"I can't believe it!" said Ferrer. "You're alive!" Hastily he moved to the far side of the room. The place was already wet and he dreaded the thought of what might happen if Pip managed to sit up. The sick man didn't look dangerous but one could never tell what he might do if he recuperated.

"Help! Don't let him touch me! I don't want to die!" Pip's voice rose to a shrill squeak.

"Shut up! How much of this insanity do you think I can take? I'm a human being."

Pip turned his head. "Who are you?"

Ferrer only sniffled and groaned.

"At least you aren't Peru." Pip shivered, looked down at himself. "What happened to me? Where am I?" He laid his head back on the floor, closed his eyes and didn't open them for two days. Then he arose and walked out into the sunshine. It took him a few more hours to completely dry out. The brainwashing might have done him some good or it could be that his unusual psyche needed a few days to assimilate what had happened in the desco camp.

"How did I get here?" he said to Ferrer who sat beside him on the beach.

"Why aren't you dead? I can't for the life of me figure out just exactly what you are."

"You don't look very ordinary," said Pip. "You must be some kind of mutant."

"There's only one answer. You people have got to be the result of plant-animal experiments. Those bloody fools! No matter how many laws were passed, there were always criminals hiding in basements committing unspeakable crimes."

"I wish we spoke the same language," said Pip. "I'd tell you about Peru. I told Kadooka and the women but they think I'm still delirious. Are you planning to marry DeLoona? She wants you, you know. You could do worse. She's very attractive, though LaLa is the better of them. Hey, that gives me an idea. You can have her too and then she'll be off my back."

"Shut up," Ferrer said wearily. "I can't understand a clicking word you're saying."

Pip reached out and pinched a brown arm, felt of the yellow hair, stared into the dark eyes. "We're built exactly the same but we don't look much alike. Besides your color and texture, you're shorter and heavier. How do you account for that?"

"Stop examining me as if I were a specimen in a jar. And cease seeming intelligent. It can only make my job more difficult. It's imperative for me to keep it in mind that you're inferior and without redeeming value."

Pip stood up, went back to the cave and returned with the wig. To Ferrer it looked like a shrunken, disgusting scalp. Flattening it out Pip suddenly stuck it on the human's head.

Ferrer opened his mouth to shriek in horror at the thought of the filthy item touching him. His hands went up to tear the thing away but all at once they stopped in mid-air. His eyes crossed as he tried to see different objects simultaneously. Within moments he was rolling about on the beach in a frenzy of delight.

In alarm Pip chased him, held him down and retrieved his property.

"What happened?" said Ferrer, coming to his senses. He was gasping for breath. "What is that thing? Where did you get it?"

"Next thing you know you'll be falling out of your tree. No more for you, man. I thought you were different but now I know it."

"I'm amazed!"

"This is supposed to provide some calm, quiet pleasure, not an orgy. It would be better if you didn't try it again." Pip went back to the cave and took his pelt with him.

They were all so agreeable! So thought Ferrer while he made his preparation to leave. Not civilized, no never that, but there was a sublimity in the quality of their existence; except for Kadooka who lived in the biggest shack with his wife and children and who came down several times daily to see if anybody was taking advantage of his sisters. As if anybody would!

It was better not to say good-bye, in case someone misunderstood or had hard feelings, so he sneaked away before daylight one morning. He wore heavy plant skins and carried a stone javelin with a point sharp enough to burst a fruit just by touching it and pressing a bit. He had no confidence in his future but hoped strength would come.

The weather was foul these days, hot and muggy with occasional sunrays burning individual leaves hot enough to cause them to smoke. Only in a general way did Ferrer know where the signal station was but he reasoned that if he walked in the right direction long enough he ought to find it. Certainly he would have to go to the ground sooner or later but not just yet. It was bad enough up here among trees and trailings of bridges without going down where larger things roamed. Not that anything down there could be any bigger than the blue steeple sentry he had already confronted.

Thoughts of the creature made him brood. Why did Earth have to be like a zoo? Why couldn't it be nearly empty of life as he had always been taught? They lied to him in Laredo. Back home where his very being had begun, they told him a pack of lies. Earth was a menagerie while they taught that it was an overgrown wasteland with nothing in it but poisonous flora and small, murderous denizens.

For thousands of years no human being had walked on the planet. That's what they told him. Every living person had been lifted off in one of the ships. There was the big exodus and nobody wanted to stay behind in the ugliness and loneliness.

Perhaps the scientists were to blame. Untrustworthy iconoclasts! Obviously and plainly they had done more in their labs than just mess around mixing human and plant cells. As surely as Ferrer Burgoyne was an astronaut from space, Pip, DeLoona and the others were descendants of those hidden, forbidden experiments.

Maybe all of Earth was an experiment designed to give man a stepping stone to the stars. He was out there now, not exactly thriving on utopian globes but there were enough livable places to go around. Of course it took a great deal of money and time to locate the really nice places.

The steeples had made it possible for man to go to the stars. He built them thousands of miles up into the sky and then developed the drive that took him to the lights. A mixed blessing were the skyscrapers. First one, then dozens, then hundreds all sticking out into the endless night like beacons. Everyone went away and the silence on the home world was deafening. For a while. Out of obscurity things began to creep, crawl, fly and walk, things hidden since the species of man constructed his first weapons. There was no one to stop them from flourishing now, no one to say they couldn't grow and be openly active in their environment.

Now there was but one steeple remaining that could accommodate a landing craft. No one ever landed a ship on the ground, and after the last steeple became unsuitable man would never venture onto his home world again. It wasn't nostalgia that made the powers on Laredo come up with Project Deep Green. Laredo wasn't large or hospitable enough so why not do a little meddling with Earth? After all it was much closer than all the other worlds.

There was a chemical called Deep Green that could be sprayed from each of the steeples. It would cause certain flora and fauna to die. Effective for about twenty years, Deep Green could make Earth habitable once more for civilized human beings.

Feeling low and out of sorts, Ferrer stepped onto a leaf and glanced down. All he could see, other than the shaggy bridge, was a green ocean stretching for miles in every direction. After Deep Green was launched from the steeples all this would disappear. It would wither and fall into dust, the tree in which he stood, the forest below, the bridge. Everything living in the steeples would die, likewise the things in the trees, on the bridges and on the ground, with the exception of small life forms essential to the planet's survival. In five years' time there would be nothing here but surface grass, moss, fungi, small life, not much more. As for the steeples, they would be as barren and naked as the days when they were first constructed tier by tier.

It would be better when this wild frontier was all gone. So Burgoyne told himself. He stepped back into the protection of the tree foliage as a shadow swept down from the sky and flew under the bridge. It was a black scrate in full flight. Glistening in the sunlight it passed near to the tree where Ferrer hid and watched. The claws tucked under its belly reminded him of the great scoops on the tractors at home. The eyes were glittering bowling balls in the huge head. Slowly the bird swung in the sky, not hunting for food because it would do that out over the ocean where fish grew large enough to satisfy its appetite. Rarely did a scrate go for anything living on a bridge.

The creatures were too strong and savage and their taste was not the best.

Ferrer spent most of the day climbing down to the ground. At great height it was a relatively easy task but the lower he went the larger and farther apart grew the limbs. The foliage was less dense so that at times he had to jump farther than he liked. At last he abandoned the tree altogether and slid down a reed.

Fifty feet from the ground the last of his plant skins wore away. By the time he was preparing to leap onto what looked like a mound of moss he was scraped and bleeding in several places. Perspiring, naked, clinging to a thorny protrusion on the reed, he stared about him with waning enthusiasm. Not enough light filtered down through the overgrowth. Even though it was near time for dusk it shouldn't be this gloomy. He wished he was at home on Laredo where men lived like men.

Chapter 9

Knowing that Earth would one day be his, Peru stood on a high place and surveyed his domain. Somehow he was disappointed in what he saw. There was too much abandonment and wild growing with no control or systematic management. There wasn't enough agony or cross purpose. Everything tended to mind its own business, from the lowest crocus in the flatlands to the foolish men living in treetops.

He was in a tree himself and still inhabited the shell of the dead woman-hater called Lampla. It wasn't difficult to manipulate parts of the brain and thereby initiate movement but usually he made use of extensions of himself. There wasn't much of Lampla left in the husk that walked and talked. Mostly it was yellow and red matter over which Peru exercised total command. As for his real self, it had grown a bit but not that much and was only slightly visible to a human eye. Growth could be measured according to how many brain cells he had stolen from his victims. If his aspirations became reality there would come a day when he was so intelligent and had acquired so much wisdom that he might take up quite a bit of space, say as much as one of the larger predators on this world.

Now he let rain fall on him and then became annoyed when a piece of the body fell away into the undergrowth below. He filled in the missing area along the left ribs with material of his own making and tightened the entire edifice. By gazing into a clear pool of water captured in a leaf he was able to structure his facial features as he wished. Then he began climbing down from limb to limb until he was near the ground.

Nearby gasping sounds attracted his attention and he looked around in time to see a brown man with fair hair preparing to jump from a reed onto an anthill.

"Better not do that," he called. "The ants in that mound are savage and they're six inches long."

Red of face, more annoyed than frightened, Ferrer Burgoyne glanced up and saw a handsome man who wore clean skins and an amiable expression. "I'm too tired to climb back up but I don't like the looks of the ground down there," he said.

Peru's interest was instantly piqued. The language was unfamiliar to him. He spoke anyway, in case this creature was sufficiently intelligent to comprehend his tones of caution and patience. "Stay where you are and I'll see what I can do." He jumped from the tree, a height of about twenty feet and drove into the ground farther than he had intended. Angry and embarrassed, he spent several minutes extricating himself from the soft soil.

Scattering the anthill with his feet, he swore like a man as he flung attackers in every direction. He squashed those that climbed his legs, and in a few minutes the area was clear enough for the human to climb down.

"Thanks," Ferrer said, and then made the mistake of extending his hand.

Peru felt of the flesh, abandoned his shell and entered the strange brown one who stood staring in bewilderment as Lampla fell over. Then Burgoyne's attention was trapped by the small lump on the back of his hand. He watched as it slowly crawled up his arm. He knew it was inside him and he knew it had come from the man with yellow skin but what amazed him more than anything was that he could scarcely feel it. Its passage up his neck was marked only by a slight tickling and then it entered his brain and created horror as it prowled about with contemptuous abandonment.

Disease kept his deadly cells to himself and intended to continue doing so until he was finished with this unusual brown person. Ferrer's brain wasn't like Lampla's where the memory cells were more compact and closer together. Burgoyne's memories were everywhere and would take much time to peruse. Some of them might even be worth acquiring for his own.

Carefully Peru vacated the large brain and went back down the stupefied man's arm. Leaving the fingertip, he dropped onto Lampla and casually claimed his own property.

While Burgoyne swayed like a drunk and quaked in terror, the yellow body stood up and began talking. By now the man from Laredo had some idea of what he was dealing with. At least he realized that the body before him was only a husk for the tiny horror that had invaded him. Thoughts of mutations and insane genes were the furthest things from his mind just then. He was too busy conjuring up a vision of a red devil with horns and tail.

"I can speak your language now," said Peru. Actually he knew only the rudiments. "Would you say I'm intelligent?"

"Yes," Ferrer muttered.

"Would you also say that I'm benevolent?"

This time the man only shook his head.

"Good. I want us to understand each other. You want to find the signal station and call a ship to come from your home planet. I want the same for you. Come with me. I know where the station is."

As they walked along Peru hoped the lowlife behind him believed he had read everything there was to read in his brain. That hadn't been the case, not by a long shot; some of the language, Burgoyne's mission at the signal station, a few tantalizing images of spaceships and the world of Laredo—for the moment that was what Peru knew about the stranger. He planned to know more, planned to learn everything the man had to teach before his demise.

Things rushed upon them from the forest but the infection was fearless and even took some of the more savage ones by their throats. The rest he discouraged by poking Ferrer's javelin in their faces.

An inverted cone of shiny silver about thirty feet high, the station sat in a relatively clear space in a small vale. Originally it had been built on a mountaintop but time altered the structure of the land. Every several months the powerful pod in the structure's internals initiated a spraying of the immediate exterior with a mild defoliant that prevented the jungle from covering it over. It had been a while since the sprayer did its job and now an arachnid lived in a net-like web over the building.

The leggy creature's body was two feet in diameter, brown, ridged and glistening. As the two men signaled their approach around a bend in the brush, she sped to the top of her web, made certain she had her target in her sights and then leaped sixty feet through the air to land on Peru's chest.

She knocked him down, ate off his arm, screamed when he used the javelin to sever one of her legs. Determining in a flash that she had met more than her match in this four-legged monstrosity that remained active and strong even after it was mutilated, she made another admirable leap that saved her life. Straight into a clump of dense foliage she plunged while the whistling javelin missed her fat globe by a hair.

The arm she swallowed did her no harm. Her cellular makeup was such that Peru's filth couldn't damage her, not even to the extent of giving her a bellyache. Away from the scene she fled to go in search of a good place to build another web.

Meanwhile Ferrer Burgoyne shook and trembled to see Peru grow himself another arm. "What do you want me to do?" he said. At the moment he didn't care if he lived or died. It was simply too much. The largest native on Laredo was a four-eyed crinker eight inches long. Never in his life had Ferrer been threatened by anything other than a human, a machine or plain bad fortune.

"What do I want you to do?" said Peru. "Your job, sir." Another arm fully in place, he straightened his human form, tightened the muscles inside it, even patted down his curly hair. He knew just how much he disturbed the man with his mundane movements. Also he didn't want Burgoyne to realize that he didn't know how to open or operate the station.

The web got in Ferrer's way and he almost wept as he fought his way through it. Why didn't the carnivores on this planet ever dispose of their garbage? Why did they always leave bones and other debris hanging about to stink things up?

Finally he reached the door and cautiously placed his palms

flat on it. The computer inside measured the heat he generated
and ran a quick blood type on him. In a few minutes the door
swung open. Dust rose and settled but it was outside the panel.
Inside was sterility, stillness and the steady hum of machinery
almost immortal.

Peru didn't go in. He had a phobia about small places and
the building was only large enough to accommodate several
machines and a few people. "Don't think about locking me out
and staying in there," he said. "You'll starve and I can probably
get in through a crack anyhow."

"I have to shut the door. The computers won't activate the
communications center in the steeple if it's open."

"Go ahead and shut it." Peru walked away, sat down on a
stump several yards farther and waited. He knew the message
Burgoyne was sending. Laredo Base was being requested to
send a rescue ship. It mustn't dock in the steeple but was to
orbit and send a small craft directly to the station. A postscript:
bring plenty of weapons and be on the lookout for a man with
yellow skin.

With a chuckle the infection rocked back and forth on the
stump. How interesting had been that image of Laredo in Burgoyne's brain. Not the place. That was dull. But the populace
was something else. Intelligent, well-bred, technologically
trained. They had vehicles capable of traveling anywhere in
the galaxy which happened to be teeming with all kinds of
intelligent life. Inferior to him, naturally, but intelligent all the
same. Conquest was beginning to look like an attractive feather
in his cap.

While he leaned back and dreamed of a pleasant future, it
occurred to him that Burgoyne was taking an uncommon
amount of time to send off a simple space message. Not even
the old-time radios had been that slow.

Hopping to his feet, whistling a cheerful tune, he walked
over to the station door and rapped on it. He waited and waited,
rapped some more, listened and finally realized Burgoyne
wasn't coming out. At least not this way. Wondering if the
terrified soul had done away with himself, he walked all around
the outside of the building until he came to another smaller
door near the ground. Stuck in the crack was a long yellow

hair. The perfidy of humankind could be read in that single strand. Burgoyne had sent his blasted message and then scooted out the back exit. Even now he was plunging through the jungle at breakneck speed and would most likely terminate in the jaws of some predator.

Peru didn't really care. Except for the pleasure of killing the brown idiot he had lost little. Here he would wait until the craft landed to pick up the stray named Burgoyne. Surely the crewmen wouldn't object to taking a stranger in the stead of their intended passenger, but if they did object the stranger knew how to change their minds. He had a goal now. Rather than sporadic killing he was being offered a true profession. He would be an astronaut and go to all the worlds out in space. First he would stop at Laredo, learn all there was to learn, spread a little mayhem, enjoy his existence. Hadn't he read somewhere in the mind of one of his victims that the purpose of life was to enjoy it?

Chapter 10

Ferrer's fear for his life was continual and hadn't just begun after his escape from Peru. It was true, though, that every time he thought of the yellow maniac his terror substantially increased. His was an unconscious revulsion to filth and contamination besides an obvious desire not to be dominated or destroyed.

As he ran through the incomparable forest his nakedness served to heighten his sense of helplessness and peril. His skin was vulnerable to nearly everything touching it, unlike Pip and the others who had exteriors that were smooth and tough. He had seen them ripped by heavy thorns and briars yet they came away with only superficial scratches.

Practically everything existing here was a threat to a human being. Besides the large and generally hostile fauna and the endless entanglements of thorns and thistles, there were gurgling chuckholes that seemed to be inviting him to plunge into them. There was a russet-colored, ropelike thing that appeared to occupy a great deal of his environment and he mistook it for a vine or root. Then it writhed and he knew it was alive. There must have been yards of it coiling and stretching up into trees and back down again, lurking in the green, an endless serpent or some similar horror.

The realization came to Ferrer that no matter how cautiously he traveled he hadn't a hope of surviving in this savage frontier. No sooner did he make such an admission to himself than the tramping sound of a denizen reached his ears. Abruptly he halted and backed into a clump of bushes.

It hadn't occurred to him to check the territory behind him. The source of his fear lay ahead. He didn't think of it until he heard light breathing over his shoulder. By then the stomping sound ahead had given way to a grunting, snorting creature with a feral eye and a body as big as an elephant. It had an alligator-like head while the rest of it resembled a mound of multi-colored, hairy spheres.

With sinister breathing at his back and potential death in front of him, Ferrer stopped thinking and closed his eyes. That was too fearsome so he opened them again. The animal thrashed about in the clearing for a while, within the man's plain view, and then it ran headlong into a tree. Again and again it repeated its action, sending bark and wood splinters flying.

In spite of his fear Ferrer knew the thing was merely scratching its forehead. The tree was too large and sturdy to sustain real damage and finally the denizen waddled away to find a rougher scratching post.

A hand closed on his shoulder but he didn't cry out. At least it wasn't a mindless creature behind him ready to rip off his top. It might be Peru, though, which would be almost as bad.

DeLoona patted his shoulder, stepped past him and beckoned to him to follow. She didn't even give him time to react or voice his relief. Through the woods they ran until at last she stopped and found him a suitable garment. It was a bulbous plant dressed in gossamer silver. DeLoona stripped away a few shiny layers, handed them to Ferrer and made motions to indicate that he should wrap them about his waist and through his legs. She spoke softly at the same time but he comprehended only her gestures. All he really cared about was that she had come after him. The sight of her tall, too thin body didn't offend him at all.

Feeling better with clothes on, he followed her and obeyed her every gesture. He was surprised when they crept through a dense patch of shrubbery and came upon the tree. Had he been on his own and had he survived long enough he would have taken another direction and become lost.

DeLoona walked along the base of the gigantic growth until she found a sturdy dangling vine. Standing back, she tossed her javelin high and impaled it in a thick knot some fifty feet up. Then she took to the vine like a gymnast, hand over hand, onward and steadily upward at a rapid pace until she came to the place where her weapon was embedded. Pulling it free and making a loop in the vine so she could stand in it with one foot, she reared back and flung her javelin even higher. Then she climbed after it.

At least Ferrer could do the same. Feeling like a monkey or something even lower down the scale, he attained dizzy heights and was grateful that they didn't make him sick. DeLoona showed him where to find edible nuts and seeds. Berry vines twined around limbs, and here and there large fruit grew. The tree was a veritable orchard.

All day they climbed but as soon as the light waned so did DeLoona's vigor. Somewhat like the flora sprouting everywhere, she became lackluster and weary with the setting of the sun. They camped in an ivy cave and slept until dawn at which time they continued their journey.

Kadooka wasn't happy to see him. To his sister he said, "I thought I told you to let him go and forget him. Didn't I say he was a loser?"

"Didn't I tell you I want him for my husband?"

"Then you'd better look forward to being a young widow. Where did you find him?"

"On the ground."

"What was he doing down there?"

"Maybe trying to find his tribe."

"Good, and I hope he succeeds next time." Kadooka scowled at her. "I promised Ma I'd look out for you."

"She didn't tell you to be so possessive you run off every man who looks at me."

"Possessive! Of course I'm not that!"

"It isn't even a harmless kind of possessiveness. You hate it when any man likes me or LaLa. When are you going to face the fact that we're not little girls anymore? Why don't you concentrate on your family and leave us alone?"

"I made a promise and I'm keeping it. You're not going to marry some brown freak!"

The brown freak was in his cave trying to make himself a better pair of pants out of tougher plant skin. He was also trying to convince Pip that the other should accompany him back to the signal station.

"I have to go back," he said to his curious but amiable companion. "I doubt if Peru will still be there but I have to take the chance, otherwise I might not get off this Godforsaken planet for a while."

Pip frowned, smiled a finally blue smile and showed him how to make trousers.

"This place is fit only for animals, and I mean that in the worst way," said Ferrer. "You ought to see Laredo. I might be tempted to take you back with me but I'm afraid you'd give everyone a disease." All at once he felt of his own forehead. He wished he had a mirror so he could see his tongue. Actually he felt quite well but refused to believe he was. He checked his hands and feet for fungus, ran his fingers across his scalp in search of vermin.

"Laredo isn't as colorful as Earth," he said. "It's gray most of the time because there are shields in the sky around the city. They keep us warm and allow us to have an atmosphere. Outside the city is just a lot of desert. Funny thing—it's gray too. I guess that's just the planet's natural color. Of course the orbiting shields have something to do with it but they're necessary since Laredo can't sustain life all by itself. Earth used to be like our hothouse. Whenever we ran out of something, like bees or worms, we came back here to pick up some."

Pip listened politely. With an amused expression he watched the strange one botch the manufacturing of his own drawers.

"What about this murderer called Peru?" Ferrer said, searching his companion's face for some sign of understanding. "Peru," he repeated. He made a gruesome face, stuck out his tongue and drooled, held up one arm and with the other made motions of something dripping on the ground.

Gradually Pip's attention was captured. With an intent expression he sat up straight and stared hard at Ferrer.

"Ah, so you've seen him!" Burgoyne stood up, spread his

arms and legs and lurched a bit. "He's the one!" he said to
Pip. "That's he! He thinks he's so fine but the very sight of
him makes you want to scream." Sitting down again, he shook
his head. "No need to worry. We'll never see that buzzard
again, not even when we go down to the signal station." He
reached out and patted Pip's arm. Again he made a face to
indicate that he was talking about Peru. Then he used two
fingers to walk up his arm and up his neck. He tapped his head
to tell Pip that Peru had gone inside his brain. While the other
stared in comprehension he showed how the monster had come
out of him again and concluded his mime by revealing how
he had run away.

Pip's interest didn't seem to want to fade. Over and over
again he felt Ferrer's arm and neck, scrutinized his little dark
eyes and even pried open the human's lips so he could examine
the inside of his mouth.

Shaking his head as if he couldn't believe it, he finally
appeared to face the fact that the man from Laredo had been
in close contact with Peru and lived to tell about it.

After a few days of rest and relaxation Ferrer was ready to
go bear hunting. Not literally of course. He wasn't aware that
Pip planned to take him ornad hunting.

The two men and women sneaked away to crawl along one
of the great limbs of the tree and to see what the bridge monster
was up to at the moment. Ferrer agreed to go along because
he didn't know where they were going and because Pip let him
have a few minutes with the wig. After he rolled about on the
beach for the allotted time Pip retrieved his property and stuffed
it in his belt. Then away they went to do battle with the devil
who in this case was green and in possession of one hound-
dog ear.

The ornad had a girlfriend with him and when three of the
four saw her they blanched and tiptoed back to the safety of
foliage. As for Ferrer, he was so undone by what he observed
and the realization that the three intended to confront the monsters that he sank to his hands and knees and rapidly crawled
away.

From a place of concealment he watched the proceedings,
intending to bolt at the first sign of hostility from anything or

anyone. He didn't care that DeLoona came back to find him and then patted him on the head with a consoling hand. Rather, he cared but couldn't make his body rise up and do the manly thing, which was at least to stand by his companions. But they were accustomed to such spectacles while he was not. Ornads must be as familiar to them as breakfast or a sunset while the sight of one of them froze his elegant blood.

The three held a conversation while he listened from afar and failed to comprehend. LaLa was helping because she loved Pip, and DeLoona was there because Pip had agreed to help her civilize Brownie.

"This is all a mistake," said DeLoona, peering out at the bridge from her hiding place in the foliage.

"Yeah, I know," said Pip.

"What's that blue creature with him? I've never seen her before."

"I have. I don't know what she is but her regular mate is twice as big as she is. They live way up on the bridges we can't see."

"What's she doing down here?" said DeLoona.

"I don't know. Every so often she falls down here."

"You mean flies."

"No, I don't think so. She hasn't any wings. I think she jumps."

"Ugh! Just plain ugh! You aren't really going out there, are you?"

Pip shook his head. "Not by a long shot. I was thinking maybe we could set up a wall of Kadooka's fences along the tree out there by the beginning of the bridge."

"To keep the creatures out of here? You're doing a little wishful thinking, aren't you?"

"It's either something like that or we move the camp lower where they can't come."

This time it was DeLoona's turn to shake her head. "Kadooka refuses to do that. He says we have more rights than dumb animals. He won't give you any of his fences either. They're his pride and joy."

"I hadn't planned to ask his permission to use them."

Meantime Ferrer hid in the bushes and tried not to perspire

too heavily. He was in an insane asylum. These people were crazy. Every day of their lives they existed with horrors on all sides and now they behaved as if the behemoths on the bridge out there were objects to be casually observed. They might even be considering making the creatures move farther back onto the strands. It was heresy and the idea made him sweat.

Only a few days had passed since he sent the message but it wouldn't be too much longer before a landing craft went down to the signal station. He had to be there when it came. Together they would climb out of this zoo and make plans to defoliate the entire place.

He squatted, sweated and brooded. They wouldn't make any mistakes on Laredo nor would the pilots in the ship make any. They would follow his instructions to the letter and never, never attempt a docking in the steeple. They weren't stupid. They didn't appreciate the danger but they recognized a warning when they heard one and he had sent a very clear warning. All would be well. Wouldn't it?

Chapter 11

Laredo Space Base hadn't sent a ship to Earth for hundreds of years before Burgoyne's survey craft was launched. The colonists weren't in need of any bees or worms of late, and they always felt better when they spoke of the homeworld as if it were rotting in its grave. Dead was dead and never haunted. Now they launched a second craft piloted by two men. Where it would land was left to the discretion of the crew. Ferrer Burgoyne's message was received and his warning duly noted, but astronauts were an hysterical sort and known to exaggerate.

The foregone conclusion had to do with the fact that Earth was a languishing, comatose invalid while Laredo led the planets in scientific, cultural and intellectual excellence.

The crewmen decided on the journey to the green planet that there was no point in orbiting and sending down an auxiliary. Better that they docked in the steeple and had a look around before going to the ground. According to Burgoyne it was a jungle on the surface, teeming with ugly predators. To the devil with him and his hysteria. If he could stay alive a couple of weeks and send a message off, the situation couldn't be all that bad.

Unheeded by everybody, there was a sentry on duty in the steeple as usual, clambering up and down enormous girders, chasing away trespassers, now and then going somewhere to see if all was well. There were kitchens, offices, labs, lavatories, gyms, utility rooms, living quarters, lecture rooms, three or four churches, courtrooms, hospitals, recreation halls and a myriad of other spaces in the edifice. Before the end, before civilized man left his homeworld, the place had been used as a city by millions.

Whing was familiar with all the compartments, or with those large enough to admit him. Sometimes he preferred the sterile confines of the man-made sanctuaries to the sterile spaces outside, even though most of them were too mysterious to appreciate. There was something about open sky that wounded him in the profound pits of his soul. It was too big out there and, without knowing how, he realized that he belonged more in a human house than way out beyond the sun.

Deep space wasn't for him. He had to have something solid under him once in a while, likewise he needed an occasional breath of air and a wife with whom to fraternize. His friends were a part of his necessary environment. All that didn't mean he wasn't curious about what lay beyond the immediate bright lights in the solar system, he frequently went into the lab and attempted to make his brain work. He desired to know what other men knew.

The ship still sat in the steeple maw, many miles above the top laboratory. There were no men in it, Whing knew, because he sat outside the docking platform for the longest time. No man exited. Somehow the craft had been piloted automatically, perhaps like all the lab machines that required no one to tell them what to do. Only the small worms came out of the ship, the white one he had eaten and the brown one who disappeared in an elevator that came back up later with nothing in it.

Today he rested on the docking platform inside the steeple waiting for another spaceship door to open. This was a new craft, a second one. It had arrived a few hours ago, poked its flaming rear end into the metal maw and coasted downward a hundred miles or so until it stopped just short of the first craft.

For a long time nothing happened and Whing was beginning to worry. Why didn't the men come out? What were they waiting for? There were sharp bursts of power from the jets lower down and now and then noxious gases erupted from vents in the shiny vehicle but no one made an appearance. Once raw flame poured from a funnel, burst past the sentry and scoured the walkway between the ship's door and the entrance to some living quarters. Supposedly it sterilized the passageway. Whing was accustomed to such treatment, having practically been born inside a vortex of gas and heat.

Finally the ship's door opened and a suited worm emerged. He didn't see the sentry whose color rather merged with the blue and black of the girders and metal planks of the dock. Whing didn't grab the little beast because he was momentarily overwhelmed by disappointment. Here was the second vehicle to land in his territory during the two centuries he had existed in mortality, and both were full of worms! Well, not exactly full.

There was a little blinking green light on the helmet of the worm's suit that enraged the sentry, or perhaps he was maddened by the sight of the door closing again. Ahead of him the small creature lumbered toward the steeple exit, in a crouch with the weapon in its hand turning left and then right. With a snort of disgust Whing reached and plucked the green light off the helmet. He didn't know it was the astronaut's radio antenna.

Too disappointed to be hungry, he picked up the worm, sped across a long metal plank and hurled his burden far out into the endless night. Head over heels it traveled in slow revolutions toward a distant star.

Telling himself aloud that he had seen enough worms to last him a lifetime, he returned to his niche beside the ship and waited. There had to be somebody in there, had to be.

It took three days for the lone crew member inside to go and see if he could discover what had happened to his companion. The latter wouldn't answer his radio and in fact all communication between the two ceased the moment he exited the pressure cabin.

Number two worm reluctantly opened the ship's door and stood there in the cabin opening. He was probably wondering if he carried enough weapons to protect himself in case the sterilizing blasts missed some predator. A blue hand came into the cabin and snatched him up before he could stab the button that would have closed the door and protected the craft. He too walked the plank and was tossed out of the steeple. As he drifted away his wide-eyed gaze was fastened on the blue monstrosity hanging onto a girder and shaking a fist after him.

Whing could fit into the pressure cabin but not through the door leading into the ship. He tore away a good deal of metal wall and then kicked in some more until at last he managed to squeeze through. Objects that weren't nailed down began flying about the tubular structure. He didn't care. What was this debris to him? The infernal machine was unoccupied. There were no men nor even any more worms but only a hushed silence now that the vacuum of outer space had sucked out the artificial atmosphere.

Recognizing a banked panel of instruments when he saw one, he stabbed every button in sight and then whirled about in astonishment as the airboat trembled. He hadn't expected it. Many times in the lab he punched buttons without engendering any kind of response. There came a deep groaning from beneath the floor and the ship began sliding up through the maw like a silver bullet on tracks.

Excited and no longer disgruntled, he tried restabbing buttons that were now locked into place. Since that had no effect he tore a few machines to pieces. Nothing that he did slowed the injured vehicle or brought it to a halt.

Back the way he had come he hurried, making broken compartment doors more broken, kicking objects out of his way. He bleated in terror as he felt the ship gaining momentum. Out of the maw the craft hurtled with its dozen jets belching white destruction, and out of the tail a cringing Whing flew to careen through blackness until he slammed against his beloved steeple.

Dazed, bruised, he ricocheted, drifted and watched the flaming juggernaut crash head-on into an asteroid on a collison course with the atmosphere. It seemed as if all the loneliness in his soul welled to the surface and bubbled over. How long had he waited for visitors from the stars, and now look at what he had done to one of their ships?

After a long rest he went back inside to the lab to think it all out. Perhaps he had missed something during his past periods of cogitation. Man knew how to send drone ships to other places but never did they utilize the services of brown and white worms. They liked the company of dogs but seldom took them along on a journey, besides which, dogs were little, furry and four-legged. No, something was wrong and conceivably it could be due to his own shortcomings.

Weary and saddened he left the steeple, climbed out onto a high bridge and went to pick a fight with the first thing he met. It happened to be a female ornad of gigantic proportions. In fact she beat him up but he managed to knock her off the strands so it was he who voiced the victory cry as she spun downward past two or three hundred bridges.

Feeling conscious-stricken, Whing rambled away to his old empty nest and lay down to brood. For two weeks he stayed there and even refused to try to find food. His mind was in a quandary. He oughtn't to have done it, had no right to kick the green lady into oblivion. Just because she wasn't human didn't mean she had no rights. In a democratic society all races should be handled equally. So if he kicked one individual off a bridge he ought to kick off everybody.

For some reason that didn't sound right. He was attempting to analyze his own reasoning, as he had been doing for most of a fortnight, when Odeeda made an appearance. Sheepish but quarrelsome, she took her normal place in the center of the nest, fussed with Whing until he moved clear off the mat, and then she recounted some of her experiences. She and the ornad had been platonically happy until another ornad, a huge female, dropped out of the sky and fell on their bridge. Fortunately she landed well away from them or they all would probably have bounced off. Anyway the male ornad nursed her to consciousness, fell in love while he was doing so and decided he wanted to get married.

"You aren't supposed to fraternize with any man but me," said Whing.

"I told you I wasn't fraternizing. And what man are you talking about? You're a steeple sentry."

"I'm both."

"Are you still on that gig? Why don't you stop being silly? You're not a man."

"How do you know? What does a man look like?"

"Since I never heard of one until you started spouting junk at me I can't possibly know what they look like."

"What's that you have there?" said Whing.

"Where? What do you mean? Why, nothing. Nothing at all."

"For a second I thought you were hiding something in your flap."

"Certainly I'm not."

"Just so you didn't bring any eggs up from the lower bridge. I wouldn't like that."

"Silly, I wouldn't do such a thing."

"In fact I don't want to see any more eggs of any kind from you, do you understand?"

"Sure."

As soon as he turned his back she stuffed the egg deeper into her flap. It wasn't the same one she had carried with her down the bridges. That specimen had already hatched and the ornad ran it off. Poor thing. It only weighed eight hundred pounds and would have to scratch and scrabble for its existence. Fortunately it had its father's tough exterior. Nothing and nobody could really hurt it.

Now Odeeda hid her newest and listened to her husband rant and rave about men and democracy. As far as she was concerned he was slightly off his bridge.

"Why don't you go for a flight with your friends?" she said, and then realized at once that she had made a mistake.

"Friends!" Whing bellowed. "Those clowns my friends! I don't go up there to play! I go up to fight for my life and your safety!"

The problem was that she didn't understand him, he told himself. The thought filled him with self-pity. She simply could not comprehend his personality or his secret soul, no matter how many times he analyzed himself aloud in her presence, no matter how many explanations he proffered. Could be the woman was stupid, could be she didn't give a hang. Probably it was both.

Self-pity always made him restless so eventually he gave his wife a break and went up into the steeple. He sounded a battle cry in hopes that someone would take up the challenge, but it didn't happen. Everyone had chosen the same time to go down to the surface to get something to eat. He alone guarded the sky. Knowing how inadequately he was endowed for the mission, he kept his eyes on the lights toward Laredo and waited. By and by he forgot how essential it was to be there in case another ship came, and back down the girders he climbed. He had a snack on the way.

There was a small, funny-looking child toddling about his place in the nest.

"I had it alive!" cried Odeeda when she saw him. "I did it! I did what you wanted! I had a live baby!"

For the longest while Whing squatted and stared while annoyance and confusion waged war within him. Surely the father of this brat had been no steeple sentry. It had hound dog ears and green spots all over its blue hide.

What was it men did when their wives behaved thusly? He couldn't remember or perhaps he had never known. Better play it by ear.

"Where's the proof?" he said.

"Proof? I just said it, didn't I?"

"And I'm supposed to swallow your tale like rain?"

"You'd better if you want to stay in this nest."

"Listen, you—"

"No, you listen! Always it's me listening! I have a hole in my ear from listening to you! In a democracy we're supposed to take turns at everything."

The infant leaped onto Whing's foot and tried to deprive him of some toes. Not daring to kick it away he picked it up by a long ear and deposited it on Odeeda's lap.

"Where did you hear that?" he said.

"Where did I hear that? From your fat mouth." Odeeda stretched in a relaxed kind of way, grabbed hold of her offspring and cleaned its face for a few minutes. "My what a beautiful day it is!" she said.

Casting a sour glance east and west Whing said, "What makes you think so?"

"I've given you a handsome son, live-born, mind you; I'm in good health and I'm married to the biggest steeple sentry in the world. Come and give me a kiss."

He did and all the while the infant chewed on his tail.

Chapter 12

Normal everyday life was adventurous enough for LaLa without her going off into the wilderness with Pip. Having been born in this very tree she nevertheless had gone to the ground many times, but not to stay. Her home was up above where the air was heavy and the planet seemed to roll away like a sea of green. The point: if Pip wanted to marry her he had to stay with her.

Marrying was the farthest thing from his mind though he was careful not to say so. Kadooka or one of his dozen children kept an eye on him and had words to say if he got too close to LaLa. He felt persecuted because it was the other way around. She found excuses to visit his cave or she sought him out on the beach, or she followed him whenever he went to spy on the giants. Like today.

There were two behemoths on the bridge now and the newcomer was larger than the original. Her appetite was enormous and at least twice a day she climbed down a string to bring something back up. The male ornad shared her food and scarcely budged other than to waddle back the opposite way to pick a fight with something. His head had healed so that there was now a white scar where his ear had been. Quite often he stood up and stared long and hard at the tree where the white worm was hiding, the one who had caused his mutilation.

"One of these days he's going to come tearing over here," Pip said to LaLa.

She shrugged and nodded. "With him coming that way and Kadooka coming from this direction you'll be caught in the middle."

"What happens if I duck?"

"My brother won't come out here after you. When he wants to, he'll catch you in your cave and beat you black and blue."

"Can't you talk to him?"

LaLa shook her head. "I've tried. It doesn't do any good. In his mind I'm still toddling around with my thumb in my mouth."

Carefully Pip raised a wide section of fence and began winding a taut vine in and out of the right border. The section was stiff and upright, composed of vines an inch in diameter. The weave wasn't tight or close together, and in fact there were spaces an inch or more apart, but only a small creature could penetrate them.

"That little fence won't stop the monster," said LaLa.

"What if there's a whole wall of sections all the way across the front of the tree?"

"You mean you're planning to steal all of Kadooka's fences? He'll murder you."

"The first time he lays a hand on me I intend to go out there and throw something at the ornad so it'll come in here. I've already told him so."

"Would you do that?" she said.

"Sure, after I got everybody else away."

The section of fence hung loosely in front of them but it was just a start. In time there would be a wide barrier across the entrance to the tree and though the ornad hurled himself against it and made it yield, he wouldn't be able to get through. His teeth were powerful but they wouldn't sever the vines, and the limbs to which the vines were attached wouldn't break for another millennium.

Kadooka had been weaving fences since he was a small boy. They lay everywhere, stacks of them, some encased in mountains of webs, others hidden in ivy. He had forgotten why his father taught him the craft. Could it be that they were meant to be constructed around a camp to keep predators away? Pip thought so.

To protect his younger children Kadooka made runways by putting up walls alongside thinner limbs, thus restricting play areas. That way he didn't have to worry about their pitching into empty space. Pip left those fences untouched but went on the hunt for the others. First he retrieved those covered with webs, drove tenants out and away and dragged the sections one by one to his wall by the bridge.

"If you bother Pip I'll leave and never come back," Lala said to her brother. It was high noon and hot.

"It won't be with him. One thing he doesn't want is a wife."

"No man wants a wife, no more than any woman really wants a husband. It's just something one has to do."

"I told him he could keep the wig if he killed the ornad. That was the deal."

"He doesn't like to kill things." LaLa glared at her brother. "What do you care how he solves the problem?"

"I doubt if he will solve it. What's he doing anyway? I never can find him when I go looking for him."

"He's minding his own business. Why don't you do the same?"

"And where's that other gink? The sissy with the locks of gold?"

This time LaLa frowned. "I don't know. He wanted Pip to go to the ground with him."

"Why didn't he? It was his chance to get away."

LaLa smiled. "First of all the problem of the ornad intrigues him. For another he's still talking about Peru."

"Mr. Stinko?" Kadooka said with a sneer. "That's all a figment. A wild dream. I've been all over the world, practically, and there's no such thing as a yellow man who drips and can make you blow up and explode."

"Brownie said he wasn't ever coming back. I mean he didn't say it but that's what he meant."

"Oh, good grief, I suppose your sister is hiding in her cave bawling buckets?"

"No, she says he'll be back because there's no place else to go." For LaLa the conversation was ended and she left Kadooka's property and went back to the bridge to keep Pip company.

He put her to work sawing strips of thick vine with a swamp monster's jawbone. With them she began binding sections of fence together.

While she sat on a limb and worked she happened to look up and spied the freak snape sitting above her. He wasn't interested in her. His eyes never left Pip. He looked more relaxed than usual. Two of his furry arms hugged his knees while his other two hands clasped the back of his head. His one white eye glittered amidst the green, likewise his scarred dome.

"Pip, oh, Pip, look at that animal!" she said and he came to toss a fruit at the snape.

"Why does he hang around you all the time?" she said.

"Because he's a hardhead and doesn't know when to give up. Get out of here, you ugly fool! Scram!"

The snape scarcely seemed to move but suddenly he wasn't in plain view anymore but was concealed in foliage with just his white eye showing. Though stronger than the people, he never would attack them. He was a herbivore and ate bundy leaves and certain kinds of fruit. Generally placid, he was good at running and hiding but could be formidable when cornered. Now he skulked among leaves and watched the man.

"Why didn't you go with Brownie?" LaLa said to Pip after they resumed working.

"Because he isn't coming back. A scrate is coming down to fly him away to a place in the sky."

"That's ridiculous!"

"I agree and that's why I didn't go with him. Also, Peru is somewhere down there and I don't want to meet him again."

"Tell me the truth, didn't you make him up?"

The question didn't annoy Pip because it was asked of him nearly every day. "I told you all about what happened at the desco camp. Every word of it was true. Peru is real."

"What is he?"

"You might as well ask me what a swamp monster is. Things just grow. They start out little sometimes and then they get bigger, or they die and are never seen again, or they turn strange. It's curious, isn't it? I wonder why life is as it is?"

LaLa shrugged. "Brownie says it's partly because of the different gases on the ground and in the air. At least I think that's what he was trying to say."

Pip gave her a surprised glance. "What's wrong with the gas?"

"He says it's poison."

"Then why aren't we all dead? Personally I think his meeting with Peru deranged him. He always talks crazy."

"Does he learn quickly?"

"Oh, he's bright, but he's still crazy."

At sundown they quit and went to have dinner in her cave. Afterward Pip wandered down to a lower limb and sat to watch the deeper depths of the tree. There was a cavity in a nearby limb where he slept every night. Hanging beside it was a long and sturdy vine at the end of which was attached a heavy gourd. Every day he practiced swinging the weight back and forth through the foliage.

Now he sat waiting for Peru to show up. He knew it was bound to happen sooner or later because that was the way reality was constructed. If there were but two moving objects on the entire planet or in the total universe they had to be on a collision course. It was fate.

How he would respond when the yellow hellion made an appearance he didn't know, but he couldn't sit by and let the creature handle Kadooka's little group as he had the descoes. Somewhere, somehow, there was a way to rid the world of the pestilence and if he couldn't find it he would at least try.

Through the leaves he saw stars winking at him. They made him feel good. Lying in the wooden crevice he relaxed and thought about the world, his beautiful, loud home, the place of heady fragrances and marvels that astounded him. He would have a long and eventful life, sire odd little children, make some woman deliriously happy and go down into his grave a satisfied old man.

While he slept a sudden rain pitter-pattered all over him so that he swelled and couldn't get out of bed at daybreak.

The next afternoon Kadooka had cranky words with him. "If I'd wanted you to make a fort of this camp with my fences I would have asked you." The burly man was hot and the hair on his chest glistened with sweat. Sometimes his wife Zeeba cut it off but it always grew back.

"Be reasonable," said Pip, knowing Kadooka was sore because he hadn't thought of the idea first. "Wouldn't it be better if your wife didn't have to worry about something snatching up one of the kids?"

"Nothing is going to snatch up any of them. I keep a good watch out for trespassers."

"They're such active kids nobody can watch them one hundred percent of the time."

A big scowl had formed on Kadooka's face ever since the day he first met Pip and it never really disappeared. Now it intensified. "Never mind that, give me a turn with my wig."

"Nothing doing. I've seen you with it. You're worse than Brownie. It doesn't suit your temperament."

Kadooka advanced. "I said give it to me."

"A fat lot of good it'll do me if you fall out of the tree and land in a swamp." Pip backed away, reached for a higher limb and nimbly pulled himself onto it.

"That's my wig!" roared Kadooka. His children heard the sound and ran to observe the confrontation. They liked the way the veins in their father's neck and temples popped when he was in a rage. "Get away from here!" he yelled at them but they didn't budge. Glaring up at Pip he said, "I've been fair with you! More than fair!"

"You're a windbag. Frankly I've already had Zeeba's permission to build the walls and she doesn't want me to return the wig to you. She's afraid you'll fall and break your stupid neck. If you have any more to say, go say it to her."

"I'll have some head-squeezing to do when I get my hands on you." Kadooka's voice rose as Pip swung away and climbed higher. "You runt! I'll fix you! You can't do this to me! And if I catch you near my sister I'll fry your eyeballs!"

Pip went to work on the wall by the bridge. Eventually he hoped to have the entire camp enclosed. It wouldn't keep Peru out but it ought to make the people safe from nearly everything else.

LaLa came to tell him that DeLoona had disappeared.

"She must have gone after Brownie again," he said.

"I can't believe that. She knows he's gone for good."

"I thought I heard you say she didn't think he meant it."

"She only pretended. What else could she think? If he said he wasn't coming back it meant he didn't want to."

Pip squatted and thought. "She shouldn't have done it. She oughtn't even have gone after him that first time. She can't keep following him into danger."

"I want to go after her."

"Are you crazy?"

"Both of us. Come with me."

"I told you Peru is down there."

"She's my sister. Please, Pip."

"You don't understand. This guy is a mindless killer. If he touches you you're dead." All at once Pip frowned. "All except Brownie."

"You see. It isn't as bad as you think."

"It's worse. He didn't kill Brownie because he has a use for him. That's the only reason he wouldn't kill a person. He's full of hate and contempt and every other bad thing there is."

Laying a hand on his arm LaLa said, "Think about it. That's all I ask."

He glared at her retreating figure as she walked away. He had planned to fortify the camp and then leave to locate his future. It lay out there in the world somewhere and had nothing to do with yellow men who had bloodshot eyes. Or brown idiots with light hair. Or pretty women wanting him to get killed.

Didn't LaLa have any sense? All his life he had been a cheat, a fraud and a liar. And a coward to boot. The most dangerous thing he ever did was to run from the people he swindled. It was true that he hadn't robbed old ladies, but that didn't make him a hero.

He slammed down the jawbone he had been using. Supposing he and LaLa did go to ground and while they were gone Peru came and murdered Kadooka and his family? Suppose he and LaLa walked straight into Peru's waiting arms? It could happen that way. The yellow man wouldn't have to look too hard for them. He was a fiend and fiends were always clever.

He picked up the saw and threw it at the snape peeking at

him through the bushes. It missed and he listened as it dropped
from limb to limb on its way to the bottom. Now he would
have to go down anyway and hunt for a burial ground of swamp
monsters. He couldn't work without a saw.

Wondering why he was alive, he raised his head to stare
bleakly at the sky.

Chapter 13

The stupid fools had done the very thing he instructed them not to do! Why were people so pigheaded? The pilots had landed the ship in the steeple, had to, otherwise where was the auxiliary? Certainly not at the prearranged meeting place near the signal station. Where were the pilots? With Carpall, no doubt, or mangled somewhere up there miles in the air where humans had no business being in the first place. Idiots! Traitors! Now what was he supposed to do?

Especially was Ferrer Burgoyne angry because he was so frightened. Something or someone had been following him right from the start, almost as soon as he climbed down a vine from the tree, and now it or they waited out there in the forest. Would that it was DeLoona, but he knew it wasn't. This simply wasn't his day, his game, his lifetime.

He knew Laredo Space Base had been annoyed by his call. Annoyed! Sitting on their fat duffs in a comfortable radio room, they were annoyed with him because he was fighting for his life. It was too bad about Carpall, they said, in clipped phrases that indicated they weren't sorry at all. So much for Carpall; he would become a cipher in one of their dull ledgers.

Now was the present and Space Base could think only of the second ship. Something had happened to it, they knew, because the homing signal that was continually broadcast had abruptly cut off. Both vehicle and crew must be considered irretrievable, and a little bit of the blame for it was being laid at Burgoyne's doorstep. The message he originally sent hadn't been nearly specific enough and even read somewhat hysterical. Base couldn't help it if there had been a denizen just outside the signal station. Earth might harbor a few odd and even hostile life forms, but astronauts were expected to regard them with equanimity, otherwise how could business be carried on as usual?

The important thing was that the government didn't intend wasting any more money launching probe ships that disappeared, therefore one more craft equipped with Deep Green would shortly be dispatched. Auxiliary boats were expected to fly over every steeple and fire a package against a girder where it would become stuck fast by a powerful suction cup. Inside the packages would be timers. Once they were all securely in place an automatic signal would activate the sprayers.

What of Burgoyne? Naturally he mustn't be anywhere below the sprayers when they went off, so one of the boats would have a rendezvous with him at the signal station in exactly fifteen days, at the noon hour. He was to attempt to remain alive until then. Base out. Out! Ferrer couldn't believe it and called them back but they put him on hold until he gave up.

Hiding in the bushes outside the station, he shivered in terror. Now and then he shook with a chill. His forehead was hot and his mouth was dry. He was ill, had some kind of infection, or another one, probably contracted from DeLoona who was forever touching his arm or his hands, breathing in his face or sneezing without using a handkerchief.

He peered through the bushes at a heavy patch of shrubbery across the clearing and then recoiled when he found himself staring at two beady green eyes. What he should have done was remain where he was or perhaps even creep back into a thorny hill where he couldn't be gotten at. Instead he panicked. With a cry of alarm he burst from his protective covering, raced across open ground and headed toward deep woods. In the back of his mind was the idea that he was small enough to hide among tall weeds and thereby escape detection. That thought came after he realized his error in revealing himself to the enemy.

Before he could even touch high grass a lasso of some sort whistled through the air. He had his arms at his sides, otherwise the loop might have tightened about his neck and strangled him. It fell over his shoulders and was yanked taut at his elbows.

He never got a really good look at his captor, primarily because the latter was covered with long brown hair. It walked on two legs though it was bent over at the waist. Its arms weren't particularly long but they were packed with muscles. The head was ugly and shaggy, low-browed and somewhat reminiscent of the apes of old. With Ferrer in tow, the brute began running through the forest, dragging him along behind and flattening everything in his path except for an occasional tough root or low stump. Ferrer tried to keep his head up while the front of his body made a wide swath in the wilderness.

Deep in the woods was a pit where several million carnivorous bees had built a nest. The hairy one hauled his sacrificial goat to the pit's edge and proceeded to throw the loose end of the rope over a jutting limb.

Ferrer felt himself swinging out over the hole. There he looked down and saw a huge, seething, black mound some thirty feet below.

The hairy brute wanted the bees' honey but he couldn't get it without being stung or perhaps even attacked and eaten by the swarm. They needed to be distracted. His was an old ploy and so he knew exactly what he was about. Drooling because he could already taste the honey, he chuckled in Ferrer's face, held onto the rope that was now across the limb and slowly began feeding it through his fingers.

At about that time someone spoke, but the words weren't loud enough to be heard above the victim's screams.

"I say, stop that immediately!" roared a voice and the hairy one was sufficiently startled to close his fist on the rope and hold it stationary. Snorting with impatience, he stamped his feet and waited for the voice's owner to make an appearance.

Revolving in the air, Ferrer twisted about and saw Peru walking out of the woods. Raising his head to the sky he bellowed his fear and pain. Desired by two devils, he could only complain to heaven.

The hairy one had intended to lower the skinny worm until it was low enough for the buzzers to smell it. They would leave the cone and fasten themselves onto the living flesh and, while they gorged, hairy would sneak into the pit from the far side, grab up the sweetness and make off with it. The strategy always worked and it would work this time, just as soon as he got rid of this other skinny worm.

Hairy tied the end of the rope to a tough root on the ground and ran at the newcomer, intending to take him by his scrawny throat. The yellow one picked up a small stone, spat a gob of filth onto it and then flung it hard. It hit hairy on the cheek and broke the skin.

He gave a howl and made as if to leap onto his antagonist. Instead he appeared to stumble, staggered a few more steps and then shrieked in agony. His cheek grew a large bubble that thinned as its proportions increased. Wide-eyed, he stood and helplessly watched. Round and huge the globe swelled and swelled and when it exploded it wiped hairy's head from his body.

Peru smiled and swaggered over to the pit where he wagged a finger at the man revolving there. "I saw you in the message building. I've been waiting all this time for you."

"Help!" cried Ferrer, feebly and with no hope.

"But I'm here! I'm your help!"

"Help!"

"Foolish man. Peru can be a sanctuary when the situation warrants, and I believe this one does."

"Help!"

The yellow man hadn't yet reached down to untie the rope. He rather enjoyed the spectacle presented here. There was he, the supreme horrifier, there were in the hole the terrible little insects that could strip a man of his mortal clothing in a matter of minutes, and there was the human fool waiting and screeching for destiny to terminate his misery.

"All I want to know from you is where the ship landed," he said. "That's all I want."

"Help!"

"It didn't land here as it was supposed to do which means it has to be somewhere else."

"Somebody please help me! Save me!"

"You see I didn't get all your memories that first time we

had a meeting. It's such a bore consuming cells. I mean there's a limit to the appetite of someone as small as I. Why don't you simply tell me what I know and I promise to kill you quickly. You'll scarcely suffer at all."

"You'll give me to the bees!"

"Whatever makes you think that? You obviously don't know me very well or understand me at all. Why should I share my pleasure with such mindless creatures?"

"You want to torture me to death!"

"Well, yes, but if I make a promise I'll keep it. Swift annihilation will be yours. You have my word on it. Think of it: sweet blackness. Oh, yes, it can be sweet. I know because I've been there. I once hung in a cave for about a billion years."

Ferrer ceased his blubbering long enough to stare at the malevolent face. "Is that why you hate everything?"

"Where did you get that idiotic idea?"

"It wasn't my fault or anyone's. If you hung in blackness it was probably because that was where you were born. Nobody knew you were there so they couldn't come in and help you."

Peru laughed but there was a sound of strain in his tone. "There's an eternal psyche that knows everything."

"You mean God? If you want to blame Him go ahead but don't take your frustrations out on your brethren."

"Brethren! Consarn you, you inferior clod! If I have any relatives you definitely are not one of them! By golly, I'll take you down from there and squeeze the drippings out of you!"

He bent over to take hold of the rope just as DeLoona came swinging through the trees on a vine like a junglewoman. The flat of her feet caught the yellow man on the rear and pitched him into the hole where he fell squarely onto the seething mound of buzzers.

Landing near the edge, DeLoona used a crooked stick to snare the rope above Ferrer. Then she pulled him away from the opening and untied his bonds. Together they ran into the wild frontier of flora and fauna, all seemingly benign in comparison with what they left behind.

They didn't get very high into the home tree before Ferrer's strength gave out. The day of terror and activity had been too much for him. At last DeLoona located a deep crevice in a limb, lay down with her companion and held him close. He tried to protest but his fever had decided to rage. Thinking of alien differences and the fastidiousness of civilized man, he laid his face on the soft bosom and slept.

Several days later they arrived at the camp and found the way barred by Kadooka's fences. Pip had constructed his fortress. The only clear passages left were those that opened out over endless drops. For a while the two banged on the vines and yelled until finally Pip came to let them in.

"Lala and I were just getting ready to come and find you," he said. Indicating his fences, he added, "How do you like them?"

"Not now," said DeLoona. "I'm sorry but we had to come here. Brownie was too weak to travel anywhere else."

"What's wrong?"

"Peru. He's following us. He nearly caught us."

"I'm okay," said Ferrer. "Really I am. I've had plenty of time to recuperate." He did feel all right now and the sight of the camp had a deal to do with it. The safety of numbers always helped him lose his fear. However, his telling his companions did no good since they didn't understand him, so he showed them by refusing to go inside the walls.

"I think you'd both better come in," said Pip. "I'll lock up after you and be on my way."

"Why?" said DeLoona. "What are you planning to do? Where are you going?"

"I don't want that Peru up here so I'll have to try to stop him. I've been waiting for him to show up. I knew it would happen sooner or later."

"I'll go with you." A glance at Ferrer's stubborn expression and DeLoona said, "We'll both go with you."

Together they climbed a third of the way back down the tree where Pip had his private little camp.

"It's nearly dark," he said. "I have a suspicion Peru doesn't do much after the sun goes down. For some reason he doesn't seem to like the night. I doubt if it's because he's like us."

"I hope you're right," said DeLoona. "I'd like to think he's afraid of something. Let me tell you what he did to a frallop."

"I don't want to hear. I've seen enough of his work to last me a lifetime."

They slept undisturbed and rose with the sun, ate, washed in a pond captured in a huge leaf, after which they settled down in heavy foliage and watched the trails below.

Peru didn't come that day or the next. On the third day he made his appearance on lower limbs, shortly after daybreak of a foggy morning.

DeLoona and Ferrer hung back while Pip boldly walked to the edge of the limb and looked down. The vine with the gourd secured to it was in his hand.

Peru was either getting careless these days or his negative emotions held more sway over his will than he cared to admit to himself. His confrontation with the mutant bees had left him disheveled and out of sorts, and he hadn't made any repairs. The small creatures were never too choosy when it came to food. When the yellow man fell onto their nest several of them ate their way completely through him, leaving him looking more like Swiss cheese than a mortal. His red and swirling eyes had promptly fallen prey to their greed, likewise his ears and nose. A few of his teeth were gone, as were three fingers and four toes. The shape of his skull was all wrong because some bees burrowed through a section on the top right, came out the other side and carried the section away.

He had been angry enough to try to destroy them but they were contemptuous of his bacteria, being immune and not in the least bit of danger of infection. A dozen or so were crushed by the balls of offal he hurled but eventually he realized his best course of action would be to get the devil out of the pit. He did but the swarm followed him into the forest pecking at him like miniature birds.

Now sickened and full of ire because of his bad fortune, he kept his head high and climbed toward what he hoped would be a fortuitous change in his circumstances.

Ferrer and DeLoona hid in foliage and watched as Pip began swinging the gourd back and forth in long, powerful arcs. He didn't want to look down but did anyway and spotted the eyeless monstrosity making his way upward.

Just as Peru stepped into clear view, quite near the edge of

a wide limb, Pip lowered the vine, swung hard and aimed the
gourd at the mutilated figure. The heavy weight caught Peru
in the stomach, lifted him cleanly off his foundation and
dumped him out into space. They heard him responding all the
way down, not with frightened cries but with grunts of outrage
and fury.

Chapter 14

The nature of the infection named Peru was such that he needed a great deal of food, not for his small self but for the shell of protoplasm around him. The body of Lampla had been assaulted and abused to the extent that a considerable portion of it was gone, but the brain and musculature remained.

Peru's unique influence precluded that the flesh would ever rot. The spirit of life, weird, and scandalous as it might be, flowed throughout the hulk and gave it motion. Everything functioned as it was created to function. The brain gave off radiant energy of a peculiar sort, the heart pumped pinkish-yellow fluid through veins and arteries, the synapses twitched and leaped like minuscule ballet dancers. In all, considering what it had gone through, the residue of what once belonged to Lampla was doing better than might have been expected.

Peru liked cooked food better than raw. Probably it was Lampla's influence, left behind like a faint smell or a subconscious signal. Infection didn't care. When the human shell around him did things smoothly, he was more gratified than when it staggered and groped, so he fed it cooked meat, squashy fruit and crunchy vegetables and half a gallon of water daily.

Perhaps his ego was attaining proportions that weren't good for him. After Pip knocked him out of the tree with the swinging gourd and he was flattened on the marsh grass below, he determined never again to be sloppy about his appearance. Ugliness and unwholeness frightened people, and in that con-

dition they weren't liable to allow him to get near them. Not
that the wretched little man with his flying weapon wouldn't
have done what he did even if Peru had been in good shape
at the time. Disease had the future more in mind than the past.

He let a week go by before climbing the tree again and
during that time he put his body back together in an even more
attractive fashion than it had been before. His red eyes glowed
with good intent when he was finished. His shape was perfect,
being large in the shoulders and chest, narrow at the waist and
powerful in the legs. His face was finely contoured while his
black hair curled and glistened. Everything was in place and
well measured.

Only after he was totally satisfied with his reflection in a
pool did he make motions toward the tree a second time. There
was a brief interlude during which he fumed and agonized
when the jumping arachnid he had met once before leaped
from concealment behind a bush and helped herself to his right
arm.

The sight of her retreating figure leapfrogging away to safety
with his limb in her fist put him into enraged stitches, but then
he had to forget her and tend to the matter at hand. Again he
had work to do. He couldn't go manhunting without an arm.
He must look normal when he confronted those moronic idiots
up there, and he needed a whole body to climb the tree.

Preparing the arm was a matter of lengthening the muscles
along his ribs, neck and shoulder and extending them to form
an appendage. He did the same with some bones in his chest,
made semi-fluid of them, poured them into the newly fashioned
protrusion and made them assume the desired shape. Then he
filled the cavities with matter of his own making.

He was a complete man once more when he took to a vine
dangling from the tree. This special tree was never difficult
to locate as it was the largest living object in the territory and
indeed took up a considerable amount of the continent. Before
grabbing hold of the ladder nature provided him, he cast a
glance about for skulking arachnids or other mindless hostiles.
Any more delays were liable to cause him to have uncontrolla-
ble fits and tear himself to pieces.

This time he was on the lookout for swinging gourds, but

as he continued climbing and the days passed he ceased to expect any threat. Night found him huddling in a tree crevice moaning and perspiring because of nightmares. Circumstance had a way of repeating itself whenever the sun went down and he had to find a resting place. Even his small self shut down, or at least superficially. His subconscious was something else. It was a veritable snakepit of flapping ghosts, bats, screeching shades and similar frights. In his dreams he was anathema. Everything hated and was repulsed by him. Invisible and visible predators ganged up on him and chased him to the end of the world. It was always the same. He stood on the flat edge staring out and down at a bottomless black pit and then the rushing mob forced him over. Down and down he hurtled, shrieking in terror, waiting for the crushing pain that would come when he landed. He never did that, though, never reached the bottom. Forever he fell and tumbled while the mob on the edge of the world above him cheered.

Morning came and he shot bolt upright in the crevice. There was a light in his eyes and a snarl on his lips. Night was night but the day was a different proposition. Here he ruled, or if there was another who claimed ascendancy they had yet to meet.

There were no gourds that day, which was just as well for the green-eyed pipsqueak with the creative soul. The yellow man was in no mood for games or other active confrontations. His night visions had been especially harrowing and left him with a tic in his psyche.

Up and upward he labored until at last he came to a fortress of woven vines.

"Stay right where you are or I'll pop out one of your ugly eyes," said a voice. It was Pip, standing behind some leaves with a slingshot and a stone held ready.

Peru sighed, smiled, spread his hands. "Have we met?"

"In a way. My name's Pip."

"How quaint. When will you and your acquaintances face the fact that you can't harm me?"

"I never said I could, but you keep going to the trouble of fixing yourself up. I figure you'd just as soon stay pretty."

"As a matter of conversation I would." The infection felt

of the fence, gauged its strength and endurance. "This won't keep me out so why did you go to all the bother of building it?"

"You aren't the only louse in these parts. But I think it will keep you out."

"I'm very small, quite tiny enough to fit through any of these openings. What you see before you is merely my house."

"So what?" said Pip. "Think about it. If you make your body the size of a pebble and come through, how are you going to catch anybody? Do you move so swiftly in your natural form?"

An ugly look appeared on Peru's face. "Do you never sleep?" he said in a harsh voice. "I can creep up on you one by one during the night."

"I'm not so sure of that. I've never seen or heard you after sundown. In my opinion you're a day man like myself."

"I'm not anything like yourself." Peru stepped back, forced himself to relax. "Very well, no more pretense. I'll tell you what I want. Then you'll tell me if you're agreeable. I warn you that if you are not, everyone inside your fences is doomed."

"What do you want?"

"Burgoyne."

"What's that?"

"The man from Laredo."

Shaking his head, Pip said, "I still don't know what you're talking about."

"I can't understand what you're saying but I've an idea the conversation is about me," said a voice behind him. Ferrer stepped out into the open and laid a hand on Pip's arm. "Never mind worrying about what I'm saying. Forget it."

"So there you are!" Peru said in the starman's language. "I had a suspicion you were somewhere about."

"I am but not for anything am I coming out to you."

Peru gave a sly smile. "Not even to save the lives of your friends? Or shall I say associates? I can't really believe they're your friends when you're planning to murder them much more cruelly than I would ever have done."

"What do you mean?"

"I was in your head, remember? If the business about Deep

Green hadn't appalled me so and captured my attention I'd have learned the other essentials I need to know from your memory cells."

"You're a devil," Ferrer muttered.

"And so are you, astronaut from afar! So are you! You live with these people, eat their food and accept their assistance and hospitality while you plot their demise and the end of their world. Don't call me names, wretch."

"I'm still not coming out."

"Then you'd better be prepared to impart some information. You needn't worry about compromising your security systems. I don't object to Project Deep Green."

Amusement and a certain satisfaction stirred in Ferrer's expression. "I don't see why not. You can't survive it."

"Poppycock! Since when does my welfare depend upon chlorophyll? You're narrow-minded in that all your premises begin with yourself and your own nature. But never mind that, I want to know what happened to the plane that was supposed to pick you up."

"I can't tell you because I don't know. The mother ship didn't follow my instructions. If she's still in one piece she's sitting in top of the steeple."

"The launcher? Which one?"

Ferrer pointed to the bridge running partially through the tree and stretching out of sight to the west. "That one over there."

Peru stepped close to the fence. "You'd better not be lying to me."

"Why should I? What do you care about the ship?"

"That ought to be obvious. I intend to go to Laredo."

Burgoyne was so startled that he laughed. "That's absurd! That's nonsense! Whatever makes you think you can pull off something like that?"

"You underestimate me. I can be sly when provoked. I'll get along, you can count on it. If there's a ship up there and it takes off for Laredo I'll be a passenger. If there isn't a ship up there I'll come back here and make a balloon of your head." Peru turned and started away. Then he paused. "Incidentally I'm not leaving until Deep Green is launched. I think the project is probably the most intelligent and worthy idea manufactured by your people. I want to watch. I love carnage, in case you hadn't noticed."

Pip watched him climb through the tree toward the bridge. "What was that all about?" he said to Ferrer who only shook his head and looked glum.

Peru was agile when he wanted to be. Since easy access to the bridge was cut off by the fences he climbed under them and made his way from small branch to knobby protuberance to indentation. There were plenty of hand and foot holds and he hadn't any real trouble making headway. Finally he crawled out upon the bridge proper and stood with his back to the high barrier of woven vines. It was a foggy day and he couldn't see very far across the strands. In his estimation the steeple was about ten miles away, which should take him a few hours of walking.

The wind was light but still the bridge swayed. It was a smelly old mammoth constructed centuries before and fortified to some extent by nearly everything that had flown past or crawled upon it. Peru's lip curled in disgust as he walked forward. How could anybody live this way?

His weight scarcely made an impression and the creatures living on the span weren't alerted to his presence until he was nearly upon them. The male ornad was in a cranky mood because he was hungry. His companion had gone down a string hours ago to find food. Not overly intelligent she became confused in the fog and couldn't find the right string to climb back up. Now the male prowled and entertained dark thoughts about what he would do when and if she finally returned.

How he mistook Peru for another ornad was a mystery known only to him. Maybe it was because of his binocular vision. It might have been that the tiny man making his fastidious passage across the fragrant span suddenly loomed enormous in his vision. At any rate he leaped onto his sixteen feet, lowered his head like a bull and charged what he supposed was his wife who was clearly trying to starve him to death.

Had his forehead connected with the female of his species she probably would have been knocked head over rear onto her back and that would have been that. The ornad never looked up to see what reared in front of him, just galloped at full speed across the familiar trail and headed straight for Peru who suddenly stood still with a disbelieving look on his face. He tried to react and did, but not nearly rapidly enough.

The butt he received did several things almost simultaneously. The body of Lampla took on the shape of a flat rectangle. It skyrocketed into the air like a missile, connected with the underside of another bridge that didn't yield very much in the opposite direction. That second span gave just enough to hurl him back down toward the ornad. He didn't hit either the indignant monster or the bridge upon which it stood. Rather he missed them both by a matter of a few yards and plunged two thousand feet into the lake.

The impact destroyed Lampla's body. Crushed and broken, it crumbled like a cracker and was dispersed upon the water. Portions sank while others floated on the currents.

One small piece drifted toward a leaf upon which a croaker sat. Laboriously it climbed the thick edge, scrambled toward the living creature and leaped into it.

The fury that Peru was experiencing knew no bounds. Rudely invading the inferior brain, he settled into a comfortable niche and looked about for a place to begin taking over the croaker's will. He grew angry when he discovered this wasn't possible. The brain was too rudimentary. Unlike a man's, the cells were small and too widely spaced.

Deciding to kill the beast and find another host, he discovered that he couldn't produce extra matter in the small confines of the brainpan. He tried but nothing came out of him. The fact was that the croaker's flesh refused to putrefy. Perhaps Peru could bore back outside and destroy the thing there. "Move over!" he yelled at a batch of floating brain debris, and then to his surprise the croaker jumped off the leaf and sank. "Go back where you were!" he cried, not really expecting the animal to obey. He had said it only because the thought of lying on the lake bottom for a billion years made him afraid.

The croaker swam to the surface, obeyed the command and climbed onto the leaf. What language had Peru spoken? None verbally but only with his mind, which seemed to use some

kind of universal tongue. He didn't know how he did it, but
he reasoned that his voice inside the croaker's brain seemed
to the beast like its own thoughts. Why shouldn't it do what
it told itself to do?

Disease didn't really care how he mastered the croaker, only
that he did. He made it get out of the lake and go hopping
through the forest. It weighed about sixty pounds and was a
healthy specimen so it was able to go several miles before
growing exhausted. That was far enough for Peru because he
had spotted a man standing beside a mud puddle trying to catch
fish with a string and a bent thorn.

The stranger was a simpleton but he was bright enough to
know croakers weren't supposed to be this far inland. They
also weren't supposed to jump on people, but this one did,
leaped straight up to his chest and hung on. Meanwhile Peru
abandoned his inferior host, penetrated the flesh of the man
and scooted up to his brain.

The croaker crawled into the bushes and lay there for the
longest time. Finally he got up and hopped back to the
lake.

Peru didn't know what to make of the man's brain. It seemed
pretty useless the way it was but he was angry anyway. Or-
dering the hapless victim to destroy himself wasn't difficult.
The brain really wasn't like the croaker's but it didn't resemble
a man's too closely either, so when Peru barked instructions
the simpleton moved like a puppet.

Dropping his fishing line in the uninhabited puddle, he found
a tree he could climb, scaled a height of some forty feet or so
and then did a swan dive into space.

Peru's purposes had been served. The man's spirit was gone
and not too much damage had been done to the body. Reluctant
to waste time indulging in wholesale slaughter, Peru avoided
the camp just around the bend. He walked the other way for
several miles. Then he stopped and tended to his exterior.
Having become accustomed to seeing Lampla's face whenever
he looked into clear water, he altered the features to resemble
the old ones. Except for the defective brain the simpleton had
owned a strong shell. Again satisfied with himself, Peru con-

tinued walking in the direction of the steeple. Satisfied he was, but happy, no. Too many had done too much to him. Revenge occupied his thoughts. His essence seethed with poison, tiny but potent.

Chapter 15

Ferrer Burgoyne stood on a leaf overlooking the valley of the forever forest, and he thought he had never seen anything so beautiful in all his life. In fact he knew he hadn't. His memories of Laredo were gray, as was that artificial world. No doubt the psychologists anticipated that his brainwashing had been so thorough that he would readily deny what his eyes and his soul saw in this place.

When had he ever felt like a part of a planet? Never before this. When had he ever really believed Earth was his motherland? Never before now.

He began to weep and Pip came to pat him on the back. DeLoona brought him water in a flower. The siren bush sang him a funeral dirge.

"I'm a traitor," he said to Pip who didn't understand him. "Let's go to the beach and I'll draw you pictures." They followed him without expecting anything. That was the way they were. "How can I begin?" he said, looking at their friendly faces. "Sit down here beside me and I'll make markings in the sand. We'll be like an adventurer or a colonist with savages. This time, though, I'm the savage while you're the civilized ones."

For hours he drew pictures and made gestures with his hands. He told them about Laredo, himself, the ships and their crews, the terrible monster living at the top of the steeple. He told them about Project Deep Green.

How much if anything they comprehended he didn't know. All he knew was that he felt better for the telling. By and by

Pip went away and he leaned over and kissed DeLoona on the cheek. It didn't make him cringe because his emotions were dry and dead. Besides, why should kissing a friend make him sick? Once when he was little he kissed a friend's pet lizard. Wasn't a woman more human than a lizard?

"I'm sorry," he said, taking her hand. "I'm sorry too that I had to wait until doomsday to tell you so. We're going to die and there's nothing I can do about it except make sure I don't weasel away to safety. For the few days or weeks we have left, my conscience won't hurt me nearly so much."

He looked at her teeth, their faint tinge of blue, and they didn't seem strange. Whoever said only opinions changed while reality remained the same?

"I wonder if you cut your hair or does it naturally stay short like that?" he said. He reached out and touched the black curls. They felt warm and soft like fur. "Don't get me wrong," he said. "I'm not romantically attracted to you. There isn't any time for anything like that anyhow, and I'm too conditioned to see you as other than a kind, odd freak. Sorry about that."

Smiling at him, DeLoona lay down on the sand and stared up at the sky.

"You're taller and skinnier than I am," Ferrer said. "You're made exactly like a human female except that you soak up water like a plant, you wilt at sundown and you aren't carnivorous. Funny but your teeth look like mine. Of course I don't eat much meat either. Mostly I ate vegetables on Laredo. I thought they tasted good until I came here." Leaning over her, he looked into her sparkling green eyes. "Did you ever go to sleep afraid that the atmosphere would be gone in the morning? Did you ever wake up and long for the sun without knowing why there was that ache inside you? Were you ever starved for the color green, something soft looking, something amusing like a young cremont, something alive besides yourself?"

"Me," said DeLoona.

He stared in surprise. "Me?" He pointed at her. "You!"

Pointing at him she said, "You!"

"Ferrer!" he said, touching his chest.

"Fare?"

"Ferrer!"

"Fare!"

Shrugging, he pointed at her and looked a question.

"DeLoona," she said.

"Doon?"

"DeLoona!"

"Doon!" It was impossible and he knew it. Given a month or so and they would be jabbering back and forth as if they had always known one another, but they wouldn't have a month, would they?

Irrevocably glum again he got up and went to the edge of the limb where he could look out at his fantastic world. There were only a few more days left before the ship came. A few days after that all the packages would be attached to the steeples all over the globe. An auxiliary would land at the signal station, wait a few hours for him to show up and then it would fly back up to the orbiting ship. This one wouldn't land in the steeple but would swing about the planet in a brief ellipse until the auxiliary was safely aboard. Then the electronic signal would be given and the sprayers would begin the slaughter.

The defoliant was fine and silvery in color. For three or four days it would blow about, getting denser with every passing hour. Gradually it would drift downward and come to rest. At once it would begin to destroy everything it touched. The tree in which Ferrer now stood would turn into an enormous stalk of ash. When it fell it would blanket miles of green, smothering, killing.

His thoughts plagued and pained him. Pip and DeLoona came to find him, made their intentions known to him by gesture and expression. They wanted to climb the steeple and ask the men in the ship not to kill the world.

He wanted to weep again. They didn't understand. He told them once more about the steeple sentry.

They said that wasn't cause for great alarm. Monsters didn't frighten them that much. After all they had existed together all their lives.

He tried explaining that the ship wouldn't land in the steeple but they couldn't comprehend how a thing could stay in the air. Even the mighty scrate had to roost now and then.

"It won't work," he said to them a dozen times. "You don't

know how the people from Laredo are. How can I make you see what I mean? They're civilized."

"Come on," said Pip. "We've got to get this over and done with. My future's waiting out in the world somewhere and I'm in a hurry to get to it."

DeLoona cast him a wry glance. "I trust you've said as much to LaLa?"

"I haven't led her on, not one bit, if that's what you mean. She knows I don't want to get married. Besides I haven't so much as kissed her and I don't intend to." Looking at Ferrer, Pip said, "How about it, man? Let's go set those people right."

"We'll never get near the ship," said Ferrer. Pip pulled him by the arm. "We have no equipment. There are plenty of suits in the upper apartments and labs, and some of them have jets on them. You're crazy! What can we do?"

"I get the idea you don't trust your own tribe," said Pip. "I hope they're not as powerful as you seem to think, but it doesn't matter. I'm climbing that steeple if I have to do it alone. This is my world and nobody is going to kill everything green in it. Who do they think they are? What kind of people are they to want to do such a thing? Don't they know I have a right to live too?"

Ferrer tried to get Kadooka to stop them.

"Listen, I never liked you anyhow, bud, with your mealy mouth and your making eyes at an innocent girl. Also I never saw man or woman cry so much in my life."

"Please, please!"

"If I rightly understand you, they're going to take you to the top of the steeple. Never mind that other stuff about scrates that carry people as passengers, I don't believe that, but if Pip and DeLoona leave you up there I'll become a believer in anything."

"Don't let them go!"

"As long as they get rid of you they have my blessing." Kadooka tapped Ferrer on the chest. "Don't get any ideas about keeping my sister up there. Try it and I'll come up and throw you off."

"How can I make you understand? You're going to die! We're all going to die!"

"There you go screaming again." Suddenly Kadooka's scowl deepened. "Actually I'd rather DeLoona stayed here and didn't go anywhere." He shrugged. "Oh, well, she's grown up and is entitled to make her own decisions. Besides she doesn't obey me anymore."

Ferrer admitted to himself that it was hopeless. Everything he did or said went unheeded. Back to Pip and DeLoona he went and helped them make preparations. He tried to tell them they would need just enough food and water to reach the steeple. There was no way he could explain. Only someone familiar with history could know that an entire nation had once lived in the ship launcher.

He wasn't totally useless and could at least show them how to cross the bridge without meeting the ornad face to face. Speaking of that creature, he was alone out there on the strands, waiting for his meal ticket who had gone to the ground on a string again.

In a bad mood, the ornad had taken to stampeding into the fence at the edge of the tree. Several times a day the camp was made to shake and tremble as the giant attempted to butt his way through the barrier. Pip's structure held and he was denied entry.

He was in repose now, not far from the fence but seemingly tranquil. The day was hot and clear and he seemed content. Actually he felt foul. He was biding his time until his better half returned from her excursion, at which time he planned some physical abuse. Now he was on the alert while his bowels rumbled with emptiness.

"Wait a minute," Pip said to his companions. He looked about for the ever-present freak snape and saw it sitting on a limb several yards over his head. "I have a funny feeling about this trip," he said. He removed the wig from his belt and just before he tossed it up to the white-eyed animal he yelled, "This is just a loan! I don't care if it belongs to you, I intend to claim it again if I ever get back here alive!"

In a flash the snape grabbed the scalp and slapped it into place on his head. There was no danger of its falling off as he began dropping down out of the tree. It belonged there. Already it was growing into his flesh and he planned to quit this territory forever. Now that he was complete again he could pursue his happiness.

Ferrer, DeLoona and Pip unlocked the fence, stepped out and locked it after them. Up the ornad's head shot at the same instant that foreign feet touched his property. His ear pointed skyward while a flame ignited in his heart. Today he was sensitive and today someone was trying to pull a fast one on him. Ready for action in a flash, he ran back and forth along a mile or so of bridge trying to catch a glimpse of the trespassers.

The three were climbing along the understrands, in single file and moving cautiously in hopes that the lumbering behemoth topside wouldn't jar them loose.

They were a mile from the tree when Ferrer happened to look down and saw the female climbing a string straight toward them. She used six pairs of feet to pull her way upward while at the same time she held onto a carcass with the remaining two.

The male located the source of vibrations and leaned out over the side of the bridge to growl at the three. His back feet had a secure hold on strands and at the same time he was bent all the way under the span trying to snag the crouching worms. So excited was he that when he spotted his mate climbing toward him he didn't yell at her with words but simply began screeching.

She stopped abruptly and stared up at him with a baleful eye. The worms were hidden from her view so that all she saw was the male bending over yelling at her. It wasn't in her nature to be tyrannical, though she was big and strong enough to subdue her companion if she wished. Remembering how he had behaved the last time she was late getting home with supper she debated over her next action and forthwith came to a decision. She climbed back down to the ground and had herself a solitary meal.

In the meantime the ornad had a fit and nearly jumped off the bridge. There was the fool woman doing just exactly what he didn't want her to do and there were the worms sneaking along right under his nose. He followed them for some miles, finally gave up in disgust and returned to the nest to wait for somebody to bring him something to eat.

After Ferrer and his companions were convinced that the creature had abandoned the chase they clambered topside and walked ahead. It didn't seem likely that anything else would squat in the ornad's territory, but nothing was certain and so they advanced slowly and with caution.

Night found them far short of the steeple. After locating individual niches in the strands, they slept.

Chapter 16

Memories came to Peru like shadows drifting from the back of his mind. They were impressions glimpsed when he was in Ferrer's brain that day beside the signal station. Brief though they had been they nevertheless were full of information. The sum of man's knowledge was but a composition of vague filterings, partial stimuli, half-reckonings and guesses.

The steeple was not unfamiliar to him. In his dreams he had gone up and down in its elevators and escalators, tramped along the winding corridors and even eaten in the cafeterias. The main elevator—the one traversing the depth and height of the structure—could be brought to the ground by a simple knocking code upon a red disc on the south side. There were five such discs. Likewise there were stairways, escalators, moving walkways and single-floor lifts.

He was interested in everything within the building but he didn't have time to examine the lower levels. What he wanted was to ride thousands of miles straight up where he would find all the fascinations he could imagine.

Bulleting up through the spire, he set the controls on the wall panel to stop at the communications lab where messages from the signal station on the ground were relayed by a primary computer. Somewhere in his mind was an image of the steeple sentry, huge and blue and endowed with exaggerated intelligence and aggressiveness. Peru knew better. Undoubtedly the monster was just that, one of the innumerable vermin creeping or flying across this miserable planet. He would have to find it and take control of its will. It would be stupid, petty and totally without cunning, a pawn for him to manipulate. First, though, he had to examine the machines.

The room smelled bland and unused. For millennia the motors in the vacuum cleaners periodically swept the dust from the air and would continue to do so for countless more years. They labored for naught. Since the last human blasted out of the maw in a star-starved craft there had been no dust here save for what was tracked in by the sentry, and he didn't come often. He didn't understand the machines, and their purring and clicking made him nervous.

Peru used his flimsy knowledge of Ferrer's language to read the instruction panels. He perused the old ship schedules, the star maps, the navigation charts. One question was paramount in his mind. Why had man abandoned his homeworld?

Only after he wandered into a library and leafed through several carefully preserved volumes did he begin to understand how humans preferred to let garbage pile up rather than dispose of it in a proper manner. The steeples became huge trash dumps as fewer and fewer ships were left to be launched. Did the garbage itself run man away or did the sight of the reeking, decaying steeples dotting the world like an exercise in acupuncture gone wild give him sufficient motive to say good-bye forever?

Just this one steeple operated now. There hadn't been another that was operable for a very long time. Since their motors were shut off, there were no vitalizing vibrations being sent through the metal parts to prevent them from decaying. Eventually they would topple one by one and be covered over by jungle and ocean. The men at Laredo probably wouldn't wait for nature to knock them down. It was likely that they would spray them with a disintegrator and hurry the process by centuries.

So much for the character of humankind. Peru hadn't expected more and wasn't disappointed. It had always been his opinion, ever since that dreadful moment eons ago when he came to wakefulness in the cave, that only he was truly intelligent in all the cosmos. Now it was his prerogative to take command of a ship and go and find out if his supposition was accurate.

First, though, he must do something about the racket someone or something made as it moved through one of the large vents on the premises. He was in the astronauts' quarters looking at the decor and wasn't anticipating what he saw. It never occurred to him that anything living could be up this high, particularly when they were outside in ultra-thin air. Not that he totally comprehended space but he knew it contained little oxygen. He was also aware that every earthly creature generally liked at least a portion of same once in a while. He never once imagined that the beast whom he was about to see could survive on a much higher plane where there was no air at all.

Just before the sentry burst into the living room the disease guessed what was coming and leaped behind a piece of furniture. Quickly vacating the limp body, he crawled up the side of the couch and perched on top, waiting for whatever was going to emerge from the vent. When it happened he squealed in astonishment and fell onto the floor. He had made himself into a ball several inches in diameter. Now rolling across warm tile he attached himself to a horny toe of the intruder and began to climb.

At the end of his journey he was annoyed. The atrocious looking sentry possessed a brain like the croaker. Its cells were so diffuse that he couldn't steal the memories. There was an advantage, though. If he perched amid the small portion of gray matter and yelled with his mind as loudly as he could the sentry heard him and obeyed. What he didn't know was that his other quiet, terrible thoughts were introduced to Whing almost in the form of subliminal communication. A difference between the sentry and the croaker was that the former possessed the sense to realize he had been invaded by an alien.

What a stupendous nothing! Peru was contemptuous of the great blue beast. Not only was it hideous in appearance but it was also unintelligent. Surely there was nothing in this inferior brain he could possibly want. The creature would never even have gotten in here had it not been that the wretched humans built their vents outlandishly large.

"Do you hear me?" he shouted, expecting no reply and

receiving none. The cells around him were like small fish mouths, going through a great deal of motion but accomplishing little. "You, ignorant good-for-nothing, will take your ugly self to the outside of this entire structure and you will leap out into space. Obey me at once! You don't deserve to exist!"

Like a marionette Whing wheeled about and marched toward the airlock.

"I'll be watching!" cried Peru. "You must do as ordered! I'm witness! If you wail you'll be totally disgraced before this peer! Go, lout!"

Into the airlock Whing lumbered. He was supposed to be overcome with self-hatred at this point or at least he assumed such was the alien's hope or intent.

"Hurl yourself from the ramparts and do the universe a tremendous favor!" Peru shouted. Quickly he slipped out of the brain, penetrated a soft passage between tough sections of exterior and slid all the way to the floor where he again picked up the ball of matter he had discarded. Like a B-B shot from a gun he rocketed through cracks under doors and down hallways and was back in the living quarters to retrieve his body by the time Whing stepped into empty space.

There was a vision screen that showed various sections of the steeple. Peru flipped knobs until he located the one that held his interest. Ah, good! The blue monstrosity was going through the right motions, was actually perched on an edge of grid. Ah, there! Over the side the fool went and from the looks of it he hadn't even hesitated.

The infection was satisfied. Turning away from the screen he went on about his business, unaware that Whing's dive had been calculated and that the sentry landed on a wide bridge only a quarter-mile below.

It didn't take Peru long to locate the ship Ferrer Burgoyne had ridden to Earth. In fact it was easy. The problem was that he couldn't gain entry. The machine was completely airtight and the yellow man couldn't remember what he had read about it in Burgoyne's mind. Probably very little or nothing, since the recollections weren't there at his beck and call. He had too many blank places in his repertoire of facts, too many lapses and cloudy patches. It wasn't his fault. Burgoyne's treachery had prevented the disease from invading him again and picking up the extra bits of data.

He couldn't get into the ship. There was a big red disc on one of the doors and, after outfitting himself again with his human body, he tried placing his hand on it. Probably the ploy didn't work because the hand had no more human life in it than one of the pieces of space debris drifting beyond the docking shelter.

No matter, there would be a second ship landing in just a matter of hours, not the main craft but an auxiliary that needed some electronic equipment in the steeple lab. Essentials for Project Deep Green. Facts stolen from Ferrer Burgoyne's memory.

In the meantime there was a library of knowledge at the yellow man's disposal.

At least he learned one thing from all the film clips he viewed. There were more ways than one to skin a cat, or there were several methods by which he could get into the ship parked in the maw. A tapping code on the red disc was the only one he could manage, but he did and was soon wandering up and down the aisles of the craft. At that, it wasn't so large, built for a crew of no more than half a dozen. There were food and water supplies for a couple of weeks, extra suits for hull work, an extensive tool compartment, but not nearly enough maps.

Elated because his life was proceeding so well, Infection set the controls for Laredo and debated about blasting away at once. If he left now he would miss the spectacle of Earth being bombarded with slow destruction. No, he would remain for the time being. Besides, he wanted to be here when the auxiliary ship landed. No one in that incidental vehicle was going to be allowed to stay alive, not if he had anything to say about it. The same thing held for the main ship, once its mission was accomplished. His name was Death and his primary purpose was to be generous with himself.

What were his plans after he reached Laredo? For the first time in his long existence he could afford to be greedy. Never mind worrying about setting a quota of victims, for there was no longer any danger of running out. The frontiers of space teemed with every kind of life. Let's see, first he would behave benignly and, if possible, even inspire confidence in Burgoyne's countrymen. They needed to be flattered and puffed up so that the deflating would be all the more enjoyable.

The government must come under his control. He might even employ serfs to carry infection around to throw on people. After all, there was the matter of time to consider. If he personally had to come in contact with a percentage of millions of people in order to depopulate the planet it would take far too long! He would grow bored! No, it would be better to hire others to do some of his work, but not all of it. To fulfill his destiny he had to be somewhere in the picture, and, too, a few death screams brightened his day.

Before the last man died on Laredo, Peru would have a ship at his disposal and detailed maps showing routes to the nearest worlds. Ah, life, ah, death, when the poles were reversed how the universe would bellow!

Chapter 17

Ferrer had timed it just right; they didn't have long to wait for the elevator. There was always the chance that when the machine was operated Peru would be alerted and come down with it. They hid in the strands until the vehicle came to a stop, the door opened and they could see it was unoccupied. Pip and DeLoona were quaking and shaking but they entered and didn't bolt out the door. Then began the long trip upward.

Twice a day they stopped riding, disembarked and found a cafeteria. Then they rode another el higher until it was time to sleep. The thought of riding into the arms of the yellow man while they slept made them decide to spend the nights in some of the many lounges on every floor.

Pip and DeLoona preferred meat, bread and dessert to fruit and vegetables, which surprised and amused Ferrer. They were afraid of or concerned with everything they saw, until it was obvious there was no danger. Then they snooped and experimented. By the time they left a particular area they were fairly familiar with all the machines.

Instead of taking elevators on up to the highest levels, they began climbing a ladder in a narrow shaft in the southeast corner of the steeple. Accustomed to horrifying heights, Pip and DeLoona readily took to the rungs while Ferrer had to prep himself with silent conversations. The world would die if he didn't climb. It would probably die even if he did, but climbing was less painful than death. Perspiring a great deal, he went up the light metal structure and tried thinking scientific thoughts.

For instance, last night DeLoona used his stomach for a pillow and he had liked the feeling. The whole situation was ludicrous. Maybe he was in love with her after all. Think of it. His lady friend was a tree. No, a dandelion. On the other hand her Romeo was a chocolate cream pie.

Inspired by the facility with which the couple ahead of him moved, he hastened his own pace. If only he could get to the message center before the ship left Laredo. If only Peru wasn't waiting for them. If only he had never been born.

They crawled through a narrow vent and spent the night in a park. Pip and DeLoona made fun of the tiny trees and other plants. They didn't seem to believe Ferrer's laborious explanation that all of Earth's flora had once been like this. DeLoona climbed a tall oak and then laughingly jumped from it. She landed like a gymnast, laughed some more and then went to sample the water in a fountain. Seeming skeptical that it was good to the taste, she splashed some on Pip who howled and ran away.

Upward and onward each dawn they climbed the ladder. Ferrer let his companions tell him what time it was. Never having seen a watch or a sundial they nevertheless had a sense of knowing when it was night, day or in between. Regularly at dusk they tired and asked to stop to rest.

One morning they could go no farther without running directly into Peru who was ensconced in the communications lab.

"There he is!" said Pip in a low voice, and the other two froze.

They were in a small anteroom just off the ladder shaft. Like children they knelt below a glass section in a door and peeked into the room beyond. There the infection sat in a comfortable chair with a smile on his lips and his ear glued to a listening device. He wasn't sending or receiving messages. He was eavesdropping on communications from Laredo. The people at Space Base were discussing politics at the same time that they were broadcasting automatic alerts to the two ships on Earth. They didn't expect a response but they were under orders to try to raise the crews. Except for Burgoyne. Him they didn't want to hear from.

Knowing where another relay station was located on the opposite side of the steeple, Ferrer Burgoyne motioned for the others to come away with him. Peru was sitting beside the primary computer and would notice when it was activated but he wouldn't be able to interfere with its operation. Nor would he be able to trace the message source in time to catch the man from Laredo and his friends.

There were moving walkways that traveled from east to west at great speeds so that Ferrer didn't have to waste time. The three fitted themselves into cubbyholes, fastened their seat belts and then Ferrer pulled a lever on the wall that sent them rushing across the metal miles.

Having learned caution, he used an exit that was mere yards from the western exterior wall. Thick transparent partitions showed them the grayness of the thin sky, and for a little while Pip and DeLoona were overcome with shock and vertigo. Once they had recovered, or once they succeeded in suspending belief, they stood looking down at the swirling white and blue world they called home.

While they watched and tried to make sense and logic of what they saw, Whing came climbing hand-over-hand up the girders. He realized they were there only after he was well up into their line of vision. They had seen him right away but were too astonished to react.

Green and brown eyes stared into huge blue eyes and all were rendered speechless with amazement, Ferrer because a close look at the behemoth was more than he needed, the Earthlings because they had never seen such a huge wingless creature and Whing because he thought he had already gotten rid of all the worms in his house, except for Peru and the brown one that escaped.

He tried breaking the glass with his fist. So powerful was the blow that those inside believed they heard or felt some reverberations. They turned and ran even as Whing changed course and rapidly headed for the nearest entrance to the inside.

The message room wasn't too far away. Down a hallway

the three fled, intending to chance trying to get off a word to
Laredo. Before they could reach their destination they heard
a racket somewhere behind them that told them they were being
pursued. Somehow the blue monster had gotten in.

Up to now Pip and DeLoona had accepted Ferrer's leadership but Pip put a stop to it by motioning them all to a halt
and indicating that they ought to go the other way.

"We need to hide in one of those caves with doors on them,"
he said. "The monster will pass us by and then we can go
higher."

"No, we can't go back!" said Ferrer. "I have to get to the
message center and radio Laredo."

"The monster hasn't a keen sense of smell," said Pip. "At
least I don't think he has. None of the other large animals do.
If we hide in a good place he won't be able to find us."

Ferrer almost wrung his hands. From the beginning to this
point his life had been a fiasco. Now things were looking down
instead of up. "It may be too late but I've got to try to get a
message away. I've lost track of the days. Maybe the ship is
on its way. Don't you understand? We're doomed!"

DeLoona said, "He looks desperate."

"He's never looked any different to me," said Pip. "Something is usually upsetting him."

"I promised LaLa I'd bring you back safely."

"Bless her and I wish I could see her right now." Pip glanced
at Ferrer. "I don't know. I wish I knew exactly what he was
saying. First he wanted to come and now he seems to want to
commit suicide."

"Maybe we should do what he wants and keep going in this
direction."

"We'd be fools. The monster will be upon us any minute
now and there are no caves farther down this trail."

They each took one of Ferrer's arms and pulled him back
the other way.

"No, no, we've got to get to the relay station! I haven't time
to draw you pictures!"

A clattering in the hallway grew louder. Taking a firmer
grip on Ferrer, the two dragged him toward a room, forced
him inside and shut the door behind them. Only seconds later

a huge shadow loomed outside, partially visible through the stained-glass partition. It took up all of the hallway, and the glass strained under the pressure. Had Whing been an iota larger the walls would have shattered long ago. He knew where a wider corridor was and headed that way, leaving the three frightened people behind.

Ferrer stood in the open doorway and groaned. The beast was headed straight toward the message room. "We're undone!" he said. "We've got Peru on one side of us and that thing on the other! We'll never accomplish anything!"

"Peace," said DeLoona, touching his arm. "We'll find a way. If the scrate comes to drop the poison, we'll knock it out of the sky."

"How will we do that?" said Pip.

"How about a big slingshot?"

Pip looked about the room, felt a metal cabinet. "I don't think so. I don't believe it will be an ordinary scrate. What if it's made out of this material?"

"I hope it isn't! What can we do against something like that?"

"That's just it. Maybe that's why Brownie acts so defeated. He's familiar with all this."

"Peace," DeLoona said again to Ferrer.

"We can't do what he wants if we don't know what it is," said Pip.

"Either we accept his leadership or we don't."

"It's all right with me. I have no objections. I just came along to follow orders anyhow."

Giving him a long look DeLoona said, "You don't trust him, do you?"

"Yes, I do. He isn't like us exactly but I think I understand him. Anyhow I believe he's as concerned about the world as I am."

"He acts as if the whole thing is hopeless."

"Maybe it is but as long as I'm not certain of it I'm going to keep trying. All I care about is being there when the scrate lands in the top of this thing we're in."

They walked first one way down the long corridor and then back the other. Pip wanted to go west while Ferrer preferred the east. Peru solved their dilemma by coming through a far door. He just missed seeing them as they ducked behind a line of statues. His sense of smell was not one of his keener characteristics and so he went on by them, sauntering at leisure as he traveled about, looking at everything and perhaps expecting to learn something. Coincidentally he chose the wide corridor down which Whing had disappeared, went through a doorway and was lost to view.

At last free to do what he pleased, Ferrer ran all the way to the nearest walkway and set in operation only moments after the others buckled themselves in their places.

He never did find out if he was too late and the ship had launched from Laredo. They wouldn't tell him. Space Base was sulky. They wouldn't answer his questions about the ship and they refused to get the President on the line. Who did Burgoyne think he was? If he knew what was good for him he would get himself down to the signal station on the ground and prepare to be lifted off by the auxiliary.

"We don't understand your position and we don't care," was one of their responses. "You're being hysterical."

"There are people living here!" Burgoyne relayed to them on a kicker beam. "Human beings live on this planet! Lots of them!" He had to wait only a few minutes for a reply.

"There are no people living on Earth. The last ones left thousands of years ago."

"I'm standing here with two people now. Can you see what is here better than I? You must not launch Project Deep Green. I repeat, do not launch!"

"We might colonize that world one day, if the experiment works. Of course there is the chance that the defoliant will utterly wreck the place."

"Do not launch!" said Ferrer. "Why are you behaving like nincompoops? Don't you have any sense of decency?"

"You will report to hospital upon your arrival at Space Base. That is, if you arrive. You say you're in the steeple and our signal probes confirm. Use your brain and get to the ground. The ship will not land in the maw under any circumstances nor will the auxiliary permit you to board there."

"Idiots!" said Ferrer, and this time he had gone too far.

Space Base closed down communications and refused to answer his signals. "Idiots!" he said to his friends. He looked at
them for the longest time, stared about at the antiseptic environment created by his ancestors. "I can't do any more that's
logical," he said to DeLoona.

"Peace," she said. "It's better for your heart."

"That means it's crazy time. Okay, so be it. You two can't
help me in this. What I'm going to do may kill us all but it's
the only thing left." He smiled and kissed DeLoona on the
cheek. Then he patted Pip on the shoulder.

After that he worked while they watched without understanding. It took him hours and when he was finished he wasn't
certain what he had accomplished.

Pip and DeLoona weren't prepared for his anxiety and appearance of haste after he had labored so quietly and patiently.

"There's no time to try to explain," he said to them, motioning them toward a corridor leading to an elevator. "If we
don't get out of here now we probably never will."

At that instant Peru came around a corner outside the immediate area and kicked a loose piece of machinery across the
floor. The three heard and ducked into a closet. The yellow
man came into the lab, looked around, walked over to the
vision screen and began flipping knobs. Meanwhile Ferrer
crouched in the darkness beside his companions and felt glob-
ules of perspiration form on his body like little timebombs.

Chapter 18

Whing was in a grouchy mood. He didn't rest decently these days because the long-eared brat was always in the nest biting his toes. Roaring at Odeeda to get rid of it did him no good. She claimed she loved the little thing. Pah! It wasn't natural not to run a child away to fend for itself. There was something decadent about letting this one stay. It ate more than its share, it littered the nest without ever doing any cleaning and it tormented the man of the house.

To top the domestic misery of the big sentry, there was a yellow moron skulking about who planned to help some other morons destroy the world. Complex though the situation might be, Whing had a fair intellectual grasp of it. He had always suspected that the lights in the sky were places where other beings lived. There had been occasions when he was tempted to visit them, and only the fear that he would run out of air prevented him from doing so.

His sense of timing was defective and he knew it. There was a ship with a deadly cargo coming into his part of the sky but he didn't know when. Soon didn't mean anything to him. Sometimes he went to clean the steeple of vermin, after which he soon returned to the nest, but the interval was usually three or four weeks. Still it was soon or brief to him. His reading of Peru's thoughts hadn't been pleasant, like submerging the psyche in something rank, so his memory of the yellow memories was sketchy.

Soon meant a short time in anyone's dictionary, didn't it?

Supposing while he squeezed through skinny corridors looking for worms the craft came by the light of the sun and moon and performed its unspeakable act?

Reluctantly the big blue entity shoved his way through an anteroom, continued prowling until he located an airlock spacious enough to accommodate him. He eased his body out into the familiar void. He had to climb a long way at top speed before arriving at freefall where he liked it best. Down below was too much oxygen that made him feel confined.

Soon. What did it mean to Peru? Tomorrow? After the little golden moon turned all the way around and showed him familiar craters? After the sun belched fifty times? Lethal cargo was a pair of concepts that made him brood. Why couldn't the universe be benign and harmless, as he was?

All the way to the top of his home he hurried, then hung by his feet while peering into the heaven. Which way would the ship come? From the direction where the dust furies blew, pockets of madness that carried their own built-in propulsion systems? Why they existed or where they were going he didn't know, but they always traveled the same course, tearing out of emptiness to tumble and cavort before speeding away.

He caused his binocular vision to turn telescopic, a trick he was able to manage because of the unique optical tubes connecting to his brain. With his secondary eyes he scanned the blackness and detected a foreign spot far away to his right.

At once he grew more gloomy. The spot grew slowly in dimension but he knew it must be traveling at great speed. After all, this sky belonged to him and he was wise to its ways.

Would the foreigner arrive at the steeple soon and, if so, which kind of soon? In a minute or an hour? Probably more like half a day, that being the time it took him to climb down at his best speed to the first bridges and then back up again.

He had a plan, and in his opinion there was just enough time. Giving a silent whoop of excitement, he hurled himself along the girders like a gymnast sliding down a rope. Moving at an enormous rate of speed, he slipped and hurtled as if on grease, his hands loving the feel of metal. His home had never seemed so beloved or familiar to him.

Several hours later he hung out over a heavy bridge and

sounded his loudest, most ferocious and most obnoxious war cry. A pox on the yellow worm and a pox on the worms who were sending the death ship. Oh, yes, they were indeed worms and it would be a pleasure for him to hound them to their death.

From out of a heavy fog came a faint bellow and he chuckled with satisfaction. He needn't have worried that the other giants were indisposed. One after another came distant rumblings to tell him his ancient enemies were tired of peace and eager for combat.

Once again venting his rage and hostility in several long and resounding threats that made the steeple seem to sway, he took a firm hold and began climbing back up toward the battle arena. He was gratified when he arrived there soon.

Strange it was how the void never changed. Perhaps he had a static personality that desired a similar environment. Black, beautiful and filled with a haunting emptiness, the sky was incongruous. Dotted with blinking lights and careening matter, its voice spoke to him of vacancy and hollowness.

"I'm here!" he cried without sound. "Don't be lonely! I'll never leave you!"

Like a swimmer anxious for the beginning of the race, he floated high above his home and waited for the first beast to come breaststroking his way. There it was, old Talion the showoff, tooting air through back flaps beneath her shell while pretending to plow through the vacuum with her arm movements. Seemingly borne up by a gust of wind or a buoyant tub of water, Talion rose huge and round against the backdrop of a distant nebula. Her belly glittered like a plate of jewels.

Behind her, trying to bite one of her appendages and thereby gain a free ride, drifted Quell. Something had made him impatient today, perhaps his mate who had a sharp horn growing above her nose. Every time she touched him with affection she stabbed him. If he hadn't loved her he would have traded her in on something like the old cow swimming ahead of him, only a younger version; much younger.

Scrate was treacherous and flew past the steeple and tried to circle in behind Whing. She owed the blue bruiser a thump or two, for what she couldn't remember, or perhaps she always felt hostile where he was concerned; and where every other living creature was concerned.

Whing was wise to Scrate's ways and refused to be taken unaware. Some other day he might let her have the upper hand, temporarily, but not today. Even before the bird could burst from behind the spire he was rising on what might have been a nightwind had he been in another time and place.

It wouldn't do to allow them to know he wanted them to follow him, for they possessed contrary natures and might decide to quit and go home. One thing they would never do for him in public was a favor. No, he must make them believe the sight of them frightened him. The few times he had seemed frightened filled them with glee. He was satisfied to see that his ploy worked now.

With a voiceless cry of triumph Quell released Talion's tail and took off after his blue enemy, who behaved as if he were terrified. Talion also liked what she saw, rolled over and over and forgot to maintain her swimming pose. Tooting furiously she zoomed through space and nearly collided with Scrate who had the same idea.

Higher and higher Whing floated with his back to the silvery spot that had grown quite large. His face turned to his adversaries, he made insulting gestures with his hands. When they increased their efforts to reach him he screamed in horror and fled farther away.

They were guileless but they were also fearless and so they continued to follow. This might have been a greater distance from home than they had ever gone but it was well within their limitations. It didn't occur to them that they were being duped but, if it had, the knowledge would have served only to make them angrier at Whing.

Sometimes it was like this. Instead of a brawling free-for-all there was one who earned the ire of the others. It was more fun this way as long as one didn't happen to be the odd man or woman out.

Then it didn't matter anymore because Scrate's eagle eye was drawn to the little glittering, silvery spot. In space she stopped dead and motioned for the others to look and see. Was this her imagination, were her eyes deceiving her, or was that a foreign animal entering her territory?

The longer they floated and stared, the closer the thing came, and then all of a sudden it was the ship from Laredo, full of Deep Green, come to do away with the world.

Only Whing knew that fact, but a lack of knowledge had never rendered Scrate, Quell and Talion meek or benevolent. Like predators they closed in around the ship that had drifted out of nowhere into their midst.

Perhaps they were waiting for some indication as to how they should behave with this new brute. Whing inspired them by floating on top of the vehicle and taking hold of a protruding part. At once the others attacked.

Life without sufficient threat had made men careless. Either that or the ship's crew were lazy. Probably both were the case. For whatever reason, no one inside was forewarned of the presence of the space giants until they were all over the machine.

None of the giants was larger than the metal messenger, and it weighed much more, but out here only agility was important while bulk meant little. Quell liked hugging the nose of the trespasser and peering through the transparent wall at the worms, who behaved in an agitated manner. Talion enjoyed getting beneath it and trying to lift it with her shell. While Whing sat on top, Scrate straddled the rear and folded her wings over the sides.

Instead of holding course and coming to an orbital position as had been planned, the craft was made to pick up speed. The jets didn't do Scrate any real harm but made her angry by searing one or two of her favorite feathers. She dug her claws into the hull and squeezed as hard as she could. The crew interpreted the shriek of metal fatigue as the hull threatening to split.

Quell licked the clear windows with a tongue yards long. The ship picked up more speed, but not straight on the previous course. It jerked sideways as Whing stomped a small jet that was attempting to broil his flaps. Underneath, Talion puffed mightily and shoved upward.

Like a bullet the vessel zoomed toward the atmosphere and

it was only then that the four giants considered terminating their attack. Though they enjoyed it they knew better than to allow themselves to be carried through the dense barrier of gases at this great speed. For one thing, only Scrate could fly, and for another they didn't wish to be burned to a crisp.

One by one they released their hold on the ship and floated free. All except Scrate moved back up to safety. Her body pointed like an arrow, wings flat to the sides, feet hard against her belly, the bird penetrated the gravitational barrier at the correct speed and angle. She had done it many times, her continued existence proof that she knew what she was about. The only sensation she experienced was one of pleasant warmth that trimmed her of loose fluff and debris. It also manicured her nails and shortened the forelock over her eyes.

The ship wasn't so fortunate. Several inches of the hull melted so that the inside heated. Bursting into the air above the world, the machine bucked and spun. All exterior vents and tubes were melted away. The mighty windows in the bridge were warped.

Out of the clouds came Scrate to see if the intruder still maintained its former speed. It didn't. Now it traveled at a more sedate pace. With a happy screech the great fowl caught up with it, straddled it and rode it downwind like a maddened bronc. Gyrating, tumbling head over tail, the wrecked vessel hurtled its last mortal miles with a monster on its back and then it plummeted into the ocean. It sank eight miles and settled into cold mud. Its cargo forever inert, it lay and was captured by misfortune and circumstance.

Above the water Scrate circled and wheeled, watching and waiting to see if the astonishing creature would surface. Somehow she knew it wouldn't. Back and forth she flew with her eyes on a widening area of breaking bubbles.

Chapter 19

The monitoring screen showed Peru nothing that went on several miles above the steeple in space, but he had a clear view of the deathship plunging into the atmosphere. Training the projector on the vehicle, he followed it all the way to the water. For the longest time he watched the hated scrate circling above the foam and then all at once he kicked the machine hard. At the same time vile curses came from his mouth.

He loathed it when his plans were interfered with, especially by one of the more mindless of the creatures plodding across this foul world. Again and again he kicked the monitor until at last it became obvious that all the knobs were ruined. He didn't care. He would never need to see anything on this planet again and no one else had the brains to get any use out of it. If he thought they had he would take an axe to it.

As he rushed past the closet by the exit he failed to detect the presence of anything other than dust and age. His body's olfactory organ had been inferior even when the carcass was inhabited by a human spirit. Now the nostrils were so many hairy openings that did nothing for Disease and taught him no lesson.

Up an elevator he zoomed to a broadcast booth overlooking sunbeams. "Filth!" he screamed. The sounds echoed around him but penetrated not so much a parsec of black space. The booth was for communication with the highest docking platform which was unoccupied at the moment. Besides, the microphone was tuned toward a dust spiral outside.

"Morons!" Peru cried, wincing as the ricocheting sounds made his tiny self vibrate inside the human cranium. "How dare you?" he shouted, just as loudly. Just then he didn't mind a little suffering. "I want to promise you something, all you overgrown monstrosities out, down and up there! After I conquer the universe I'm coming back here to destroy you! Never will I forget Earth no matter how far fortune takes me!"

Hurling the mike to the floor, he fumed a while to himself and then got down to business. To the devil with the deathship. It was gone now, dispatched and piloted by fools. Let it lie in its wet grave till doomsday as a monument to a species whose aspirations were never matched by their abilities.

"To me!" he bellowed, and then ran for another el that would carry him to his escape craft. Meanwhile he hoped he didn't run into the blue titan. Indeed he knew the thing hadn't died when it leaped off the battlements at his command. How did he know? There were untidy trailings along certain hallways and within a few oversized cubicles.

On second thought it might be rewarding for him to meet with it a second time in which case he would not repeat his mistake. Yes, if he encountered the sentry once again he would see to it that it died unmercifully.

He rode ever upward toward the ship, while far below the three people vacated a closet and ran toward the elevator that would take them all the way down the other way. Ever toward the heavens Peru sped until at last he arrived at the space vehicle. It was a cold vehicle.

He was angered anew. The metal moron had automatically shut off and now its engines were colder than his nonexistent heart. Blast! Why did life appear to consist mostly of delay? He was in a hurry to get out there among the blubbering masses and spread his special influence.

Physics didn't care what he wanted. The pile of stardrive

required to be coaxed and toasted like a little coal that finally generated the slightest bit of heat. Hours were needed because the result would be so awesome. At first the pink glow refused to do anything else but then gradually and nearly imperceptibly it became more intense. Then it turned red. The ship shuddered as if it anticipated with dread its tumultuous exit from reason and common time.

Happily Peru punched dials and didn't swear when the body he was wearing faltered and staggered. He had forgotten things like heat and air. Correcting that situation, moving with a degree of agility once more, he revved auxiliary engines, emptied valves of bubbles, recharged batteries and prepared for takeoff.

Far beneath him an elevator rocketed toward the clouds, which in this instance lay to the south. Inside were two curious people and one terrified person. The two had no idea of what danger they were in. The third knew all too well and watched the floor dial as they dropped from level to level as rapidly as the machine would go.

High above Peru, a lonely steeple sentry floated and played by himself. His friends had gone home and he was left to watch and wonder at the goings on around him.

Disease knew better than to send the ship up through the maw too quickly. One thing he didn't want was to damage the pads in any way. He had been serious in his threats to return one day and finish his work. Not that men would ever direct a craft down here again, for he intended to terminate the species. Perhaps he would reserve a dozen or so in order to maintain host bodies for himself. Unless, that is, he came across a species whose form he liked better.

Up the maw like a shot he went, speedily but not unreasonably so. In fact he was right on course and speed with all systems go when the dirty work or the cleanup chore performed by Ferrer Burgoyne began a series of actions and reactions.

There was no atomic blast, though enough light was produced to make it appear so. There was no sound because whatever was created below the atmosphere was sucked upward by an artificial vacuum that dispersed into the natural one.

Peru started screaming—more in rage than in fear—because he didn't understand what was happening. He recognized treachery though, which was the reason he swore.

For the first time since its birth, the steeple trembled. All the way to the ground vibrations raced far more rapidly than the elevator, inside which three people shrank and held tightly to one another. Up and down the girders raced an awesome warning and then it was as if the structure received a coherent message. Only the uppermost spires were involved in the debacle. The lower shuddering ceased and, to the lowlife struck dumb everywhere, reality proceeded again at its usual hectic pace.

Up top, though, it wasn't so rational. Peru was shrieking at the top of his lungs because he saw all his plans coming to naught. Some idiot moron had placed enough explosives in the flight spots to lift several hundred miles of steeple off the bulk. Needless to say the spaceship necessarily was involved.

Infection tried to speed up his pace, jammed the drive levers so that there was violent contact deep inside the mechanical bowels. Not quite up to quarter power, the pile attempted to respond, resulting in a jerking along the left side. It didn't matter. The ship slammed against one side of the maw, bounced on the pad tracks and hurtled against the other side. Bucking, denting, even cracking in a few places, the little arrow flew in desperation toward the open mouth.

It nearly made it. The sections of the steeple had been laid tier upon tier and were huge and cumbersome weights. Never in a month of a year of millennia would they have crumpled or collapsed. They did now. They were blasted at their moorings by sufficient explosives to pulverize an asteroid.

A neat section lifted off just before the ship cleared the maw. Out into space, tumbling end over end, went the great mass of metal. Somewhere inside it a small engine burned out and a ship broke into particles. A human body went sailing into the night in two hundred shreds. Among them was an almost microscopic object that shrieked, gibbered and voiced threats. The entire mass and all the bits and tatters followed a single course that would one day cross the path of a speeding comet.

After the initial shuddering the steeple stood as it always had. In a day or two the elevator would stop at the bridge where the ornad lived and the passengers would disembark. The machine would automatically return to its origin, which was no longer there. In a few days' time, if anything or anyone happened to be floating in the upper strata of emptiness, he would see a little boxcar shoot out of the broken spires and follow a path to nowhere.

Meanwhile Whing circled his one-time home and brooded. As a man he comprehended that great tragedies had been avoided by someone's reckless courage. Never did it enter his mind that anything had been wreaked by worms and in fact he considered that somewhere in the twisted metal below were three crushed corpses. Or they might be journeying to kingdom come with the top of his home.

He was in an extremely bad mood. It was well that the death ship had been killed but he didn't think spacemen would be coming here anymore, and that was bad. Their ships were built to land in maws and there were no more operable pads left. Something gave him the idea that men were too lazy to build new ship models. They would rather just forget about one world that had always been a thorn in their consciences and their sides. Weren't there all those new planets to explore? Why waste time with one that had proved difficult?

Feeling like an outcast and an orphan, the sentry drifted in space and surveyed the ruined crown of his brithplace. This meant of course that he had to move, find another steeple. He had no intention of living in a cripple. It meant he must choose one of the others. Vermin-filled, they were there for the taking. Filthy with the debris of uncounted eras, they were all over the surface of the land. How long would it take him to make one habitable?

In a grouchy frame of mind he grabbed hold of a wrinkled girder and began the long climb down to his private bridge.

His humor hadn't improved by the time he arrived there. While Odeeda was in mid-sentence, lying her head off about somebody having sneaked a foundling egg into her nest, he kicked her off the strands. Unfortunately she took the long-eared brat with her in one of her flaps. Now he couldn't run it off while she was climbing back up.

Have you discovered...

JO CLAYTON

"Aleytys is a heroine as tough as, and more believable and engaging than, the general run of swords-and-sorcery barbarians."
—*Publishers Weekly*

The saga of Aleytys is recounted in these DAW books:

DIADEM FROM THE STARS	(#UE1520—$2.25)
LAMARCHOS	(#UE1627—$2.25)
IRSUD	(#UE1640—$2.25)
MAEVE	(#UE1469—$1.75)
STAR HUNTERS	(#UE1550—$1.75)
THE NOWHERE HUNT	(#UE1665—$2.25)

Recommended for Star Warriors!

The Commodore Grimes Novels of

A. Bertram Chandler

The Dumarest of Terra Novels of E. C. Tubb

The Daedalus Novels of Brian M. Stableford
